S0-BFB-305

Dominic held the baby while she finished her bottle.

She still hadn't closed her eyes. He smoothed her delicate brows with his thumb, marveling at each sweet feature that reminded him of Hannah.

"You know something important is going to happen tomorrow, don't you, *petite?* That's why you're still awake."

After laying her down and covering her with a light blanket, he sat on the edge of the bed where she could still see him. Her eyelids were getting heavier and kept fluttering. In a few seconds they'd be closed.

Instead of an icy-cold shower, maybe he ought to read the latest parenting tips to keep his mind off his bride-to-be. Hannah was as close as the other side of the wall. If he joined her, he doubted she would refuse....

Meet
Dominic, Alik and Zane

Three firm friends…
Three successful business partners…
Three dedicated bachelors…

But life is full of surprises, and these gorgeous men
are about to discover the joys of fatherhood—
and of marriage—sooner than they think!

Surprised by fatherhood and ready for love!

THE BILLIONAIRE
AND THE BABY

Rebecca Winters

BACHELOR
DADS

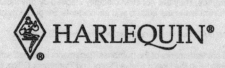

HARLEQUIN®

TORONTO • NEW YORK • LONDON
AMSTERDAM • PARIS • SYDNEY • HAMBURG
STOCKHOLM • ATHENS • TOKYO • MILAN • MADRID
PRAGUE • WARSAW • BUDAPEST • AUCKLAND

If you purchased this book without a cover you should be aware that this book is stolen property. It was reported as "unsold and destroyed" to the publisher, and neither the author nor the publisher has received any payment for this "stripped book."

ISBN 0-373-15878-5

THE BILLIONAIRE AND THE BABY

First North American Publication 2000.

Copyright © 2000 by Rebecca Winters.

All rights reserved. Except for use in any review, the reproduction or utilization of this work in whole or in part in any form by any electronic, mechanical or other means, now known or hereafter invented, including xerography, photocopying and recording, or in any information storage or retrieval system, is forbidden without the written permission of the publisher, Harlequin Enterprises Limited, 225 Duncan Mill Road, Don Mills, Ontario, Canada M3B 3K9.

All characters in this book have no existence outside the imagination of the author and have no relation whatsoever to anyone bearing the same name or names. They are not even distantly inspired by any individual known or unknown to the author, and all incidents are pure invention.

This edition published by arrangement with Harlequin Books S.A.

® and TM are trademarks of the publisher. Trademarks indicated with ® are registered in the United States Patent and Trademark Office, the Canadian Trade Marks Office and in other countries.

Visit us at www.eHarlequin.com

Printed in U.S.A.

CHAPTER ONE

DOMINIC GIRAUD finally came upon the tiny historical museum and store. He'd been told he would find it about twelve miles outside of Laramie, Wyoming. A busload of tourists appeared to have laid siege to the place.

Though he pulled his topless four-wheel drive to a stop, he didn't immediately get out of his vehicle. Instead, he took advantage of the beautiful, warm June evening to look around him.

The rugged beauty of this Western landscape was so at odds with the skyscrapers of New York City where he lived, or the Mediterranean ambience of his French birthplace in Vence, he could hardly credit he was on the same planet.

However, because he'd been born in the land of the orange tree, jasmine and lavender, he could appreciate more than most the aromatic scents of sage and Indian paintbrush in the dry air wafting past his nostrils. A man native to the sunny French Midi, he thrived under this cloud-dotted blue sky where the sun had disappeared below the horizon some time ago.

Realizing it might be a while before he could talk with the person running the place to discover the name of the owner, he decided to go off-road and explore the property behind it. He needed this section of land to link the two neighboring properties for a project he'd undertaken in the last year, and probably wouldn't see completed for several more years at least.

The idea of running a bullet train from the east to the west coast of the U.S. had consumed him for years. Now it was on its way to becoming a reality, thanks to a seminar he'd attended in England celebrating the completion of the Channel Tunnel, an unrivaled engineering feat.

Those without vision had said it couldn't be done.

They were wrong. Just as they would be wrong about the eventual completion of his bullet train.

At that momentous conference he'd met two Americans, a geologist from New York, Alik Jarman, and an engineer from San Francisco, Zane Broderick. They were men who dreamed the same kinds of dreams Dominic dreamed.

Each being pressed because of heavy work schedules, the three of them had only intended to stay in London for the day, the length of the conference. But once the other two heard his idea, all other commitments were put on hold.

For three weeks they spent literally twenty-four hours a day in a hotel suite working out the intricacies of such a massive project, one that had caught hold of their imaginations and wouldn't let go.

No longer alone with his ideas, Dominic could concentrate on raising the money and procuring the land while he marveled at the genius and speed with which the others put their scientific contributions to paper. Those weeks marked the turning point in all their lives. They came out of the experience not only firm colleagues in the greatest adventure they would ever undertake, but best friends.

Because of that chance meeting in London he was here now, doing his part to ensure the realization of their dream.

Shifting gears to four-wheel drive, he drove around the back of the store where he discovered a small barn and a vintage one-horse trailer. Nearby, a blue compact car stood parked. In the adjacent corral, a saddled chestnut sorrel quarter horse munched on some hay. All the land beyond the two buildings was an untouched vista of sage, grass and wildflowers.

The place looked lonely, or maybe he only thought that because there was this strange sense of loneliness he'd been feeling since driving out here from town. It echoed somewhere deep inside of him, disturbing him in ways he didn't care to analyze... not when he'd thought himself totally fulfilled by his work.

Impatient, he shrugged it off and headed toward a ridge he could see in the distance overlooking the river.

By the time he reached the top, his mind was once more immersed in thought over his future plans, and he reacted too slowly as his vehicle began the descent. Almost colliding with a medium-size boulder, he swerved to avoid it, then swore softly when the right rear tire caught the side of it. The next thing he knew the world was spinning and he saw lights.

Hannah Carr frowned when the sound of the departing tour bus faded and another sound took its place. Someone's horn was honking and wouldn't stop.

She finished changing her little niece's diaper, then walked outside the museum to see if the car was anywhere in sight. That's when she realized the noise was coming from the river area behind them.

Someone was out on her property, which had no road and could only be reached by walking, on horseback, or in an off-road vehicle. They could be in real trouble. Unfortunately there were no other people around for several miles.

If she called the emergency number, it would still take the paramedics a good ten to fifteen minutes to reach the museum. On her horse, Hannah could make it to the river in one fifth of the time.

Haunted by the sound of the horn, which continued its mournful blaring din, Hannah went back inside and put the baby in the playpen. By the time she'd given the six-month-old her favorite donut-shaped toy, Hannah had made a decision.

"Elizabeth? I've never left you unattended before, but I'm afraid there's something terribly wrong outside. I have to go see what it is, but I'll come right back. Please be my little sweetheart and don't cry. All right?"

It was a wrench to leave her, but Hannah didn't feel she had a choice. If someone were injured, there wasn't a second to lose.

Saying a little prayer that Elizabeth would be safe, Hannah crept across the museum and left for the corral, locking the door behind her so no one could get in to hurt the baby.

Her horse, Cinnamon, walked over to the gate and waited for her to open it. Hannah grabbed the reins and hoisted herself in the saddle. "Come on, girl. Let's find out why that horn is stuck."

More at home on the back of the horse she'd raised and trained from a foal than in her own car, she took off at a gallop and raced toward the rise, which she reached in no time at all.

She cried out when she saw a Jeep lying against an outcrop of rock near the bottom of the hill. A few feet away a man's body lay face-up in the grass, not moving.

Urging her horse forward, they made a careful descent. As soon as they got close enough, she jumped off and hurried over to the inert male who looked to be in his mid-thirties. The well-honed body dressed in faded jeans and a cream-colored polo shirt had to be several inches over six feet. His bronzed face and hard-muscled arms attested to a lot of time spent in the sun.

She sank to her knees and reached for his wrist to find a pulse. Her touch produced a moaning sound and eventually his eyelids opened. Though the pupils were enlarged, she could tell his eyes were as dark brown as his hair.

In terms of male beauty, Hannah thought him the most handsome man she'd ever laid eyes on in her life.

When he tried to sit up, she held him down. "Please lie still for a minute. You've had an accident and I'm afraid you might be suffering from a concussion."

He muttered something indistinct and made a determined effort to get to his feet. After a struggle he succeeded, but the second he put his weight on his left foot, he almost collapsed. If she hadn't been there to hold him up, he would have fallen. Either his foot or ankle, or possibly both, could be broken.

"Come on. I can't leave you out here. Let's get you on my horse. Lean on me." Though this man might be tall and powerfully built, he needed her help if he planned to go anywhere.

Hannah stood five feet four inches, but

she'd performed in rodeos and had done trick riding all her life.

More recently she'd been trained in fire fighting and rescue work through her association with Laramie's Indian Paintbrush Brigade. The group of fifty female volunteers rode horses together for pleasure. They could also be called upon to assist in an emergency.

With a low whistle she summoned her horse. Cinnamon immediately walked up to her. After adjusting the right stirrup to hang as low as possible, she urged the stranger to hoist himself up using his sound leg for leverage.

Standing on tiptoe, she eased his injured limb over the back of the horse and up onto its neck. The man made no noise, but she saw his striking features form a grimace and knew he had to be in excruciating pain. Dazed as he was, she considered it a miracle he didn't fall off her horse.

With the reins in one hand, she mounted Cinnamon from the left stirrup. Straddled behind the stranger, she used one arm to circle his waist while she guided the horse with the other.

This close to the injured man's virile physique, she could feel his warmth and smell the pleasant scent of the soap he'd used in the shower. Surprised at the direction of her thoughts, she forced herself to concentrate on the crisis at hand. Cinnamon obeyed Hannah's clicking sound and started up the hill for the corral.

Soon the man's body slumped over the horn of the saddle, yet she felt him stiffen with every movement of the horse.

Anxious to encourage him, she whispered, "The museum isn't far from here. Just a few more minutes."

Again she heard something unintelligible escape his lips. Only semi-coherent right now, the foreign-sounding words coming through clenched teeth attested to his pain. He needed a doctor as soon as possible.

In a short time the buildings came into view. With the blare of the horn still rending the night air, she half expected to hear Elizabeth wailing from the annoying sound. To Hannah's relief, all was quiet.

The second the horse stopped, she slid off its rump and hurriedly reached to help the stranger dismount. With him sagging heavily against her, she fumbled in her pocket for the key, then unlocked the front door.

Half dragging him, they reached the bunk at one end of the room. He fell into it with a muffled groan and didn't open his eyes again, beads of perspiration dotted his upper lip and hairline.

To Hannah's relief the baby had fallen asleep and all seemed well. She muttered another prayer, this time in gratitude because residue guilt still plagued her for having left Elizabeth at all. But Hannah had sensed a crisis and was glad she'd been able to help the stranger.

Worried about the man's head, she examined his skull with her fingers. There was a small lump on the back beneath his dark, vibrant hair, but no open wound. It was possible he could have sustained internal bleeding.

Carefully she eased his long, powerful legs onto the thin mattress. With all the gentleness she could muster, she rolled up the hem of his jeans to examine his injured limb. The area around the outside of his ankle looked swollen, unfortunately, she couldn't tell if it was sprained or broken.

Thankful he wasn't awake to fight her, she took another peek at Elizabeth who slept on undisturbed, then reached for the first-aid kit beneath the counter. In a few minutes she'd lightly wrapped his ankle with a roll-around elastic bandage.

Looking about her, she took down one of the saddle blankets from the wall and propped his leg to keep down the swelling. If she just had some ice! Not for the first time did she wish there was electricity out here so she could keep a little fridge with a freezer compartment.

Throughout her ministrations, he groaned several times but still didn't come to.

"That's just as well," she murmured to herself as she once more reached beneath the counter for her cell phone. Satisfied that both the baby and the stranger would stay asleep for some time, she tiptoed out the door of the museum, then called for an ambulance.

After a short discussion, it was agreed they would turn off their siren so as not to alarm the baby or Hannah's patient.

Next, she phoned Jim Thornton at home. He ran one of the local garages in Laramie. When he heard what had happened, he promised he'd be out first thing in the morning to deal with the Jeep.

After she'd made her calls, Hannah walked Cinnamon to the barn. With the aid of a lantern, she removed the horse's trappings and provided her with fresh water and feed. "You deserve a reward after all your hard work at the river," she murmured, rubbing Cinnamon's forehead affectionately. The horse whinnied in response.

With Cinnamon taken care of, she carried the lantern back to the museum. Little had Hannah guessed she would need it tonight. But since finding the stranger, darkness had crept over the sage-dotted land. Lack of electrical power made it necessary for her to supply enough light for the ambulance attendants to do their job.

When Dominic opened his eyes this time, he let out a moan to discover himself alone on a hard bunk bed inside a tiny log cabin, his head and ankle hurting like hell.

His bleary gaze surveyed the dim interior in an attempt to focus. By the time he could see one image instead of three, a poster hanging on the wall right above his feet, stared back at him.

Wanted For Pony Express
Young, Skinny, Wiry Fellows. Not Over
Eighteen. Must Be Expert Riders. Willing
To Risk Death Daily. Orphans Preferred.
Apply Before April 3, 1860, To
The Central Overland California Express
Company.

At first the words had him truly confused, but he gradually became aware of his surroundings and remembered the museum. For the life of him, he couldn't recall how he'd gotten from the river to here, but someone had brought him. How else could he account for his wrapped ankle which was now elevated! Had he dreamed up the exquisite-looking angel with golden curls and green eyes who'd spirited him away on her horse?

When he tried to sit up, the room spun again. On a groan of defeat, he lay back and closed his eyes. Unfortunately he couldn't shut out the odd ringing in his ears.

"He's right in here," he heard a voice say sometime later. It was the same voice Dominic had heard earlier. A woman's voice, slightly husky and breathless.

It belonged to the angel.

He opened his eyes to make sure she wasn't a figment of his imagination. To his disappointment, a man about thirty-six, his own age, was on his haunches staring at Dominic. Another man had brought in a stretcher and placed it near the bunk.

"Hi, there. Glad to see you're awake. What's your name?"

"Dominic Giraud," he muttered, expelling a deep sigh of frustration.

"I'm Chad. We heard you had an accident

out by the river. Just rest easy while I take your vital signs, then we'll drive you into the Laramie hospital where a doctor will examine you.''

''I'm all right,'' Dominic groaned his protestation as the paramedic gave him an on-the-spot physical.

''That's probably true, but you have a small lump on the back of your head, and you might have suffered a broken ankle, which needs to be X-rayed.''

It was one of the few times in Dominic's life when he didn't have the physical strength to walk away from a situation he wanted no part of.

''Where's the angel?''

''You mean the one who rescued you and gave you expert first aid?''

''So I wasn't dreaming…''

''I'm afraid I'm just a mere mortal, Mr. Giraud.''

He liked the sound of her voice, especially the way she tried to say his name in good French. Most Americans didn't bother.

Intrigued by this telling bit of insight into her psyche he said, ''Move around so I can see you to thank you for saving my life.''

''Later.'' Chad grinned. ''She's a looker, and I might get the wrong blood pressure reading from you. Besides, I need her to stay where she is and keep holding the lantern for me.''

Dominic muttered another epithet. He would have tipped his head back to get a glimpse of her if it weren't for the fact that every time he tried to turn or sit up, the room swam.

''I was in a pileup on the freeway a while ago and know exactly how you feel,'' Chad commiserated. ''Give yourself twenty-four hours and you'll be a new man again.'' The two paramedics helped ease Dominic onto the stretcher.

He still couldn't see the woman who walked behind them to the door before she said good bye and wished him a speedy recovery. To irritate him further, the ringing sound in his ears grew worse the second they moved him outside. It took him a moment to realize the noise wasn't coming from inside his head.

''*Mon Dieu!*— That's a horn!''

''It's your Jeep. The battery will die soon.'' Chad spoke up as they placed him in the back of the ambulance. ''I understand Thornton's Garage will be out to get it in the morning. We'll leave all the details at the hospital with you.''

For the moment Dominic had no choice but to give in to his fate. That didn't mean he wouldn't be back tomorrow or the next day to thank his rescuer properly. She couldn't possibly be as beautiful as he'd imagined.

Early the next morning, after Hannah had opened the museum for business, a tow truck from Jim's garage drove up in front. With Elizabeth propped against her shoulder, she walked outside and gave the men directions to the accident site.

It reminded her to phone the hospital later in the day and find out the condition of the dark-haired stranger who'd dominated her thoughts since last night. She supposed he might be living in Laramie, but she doubted it very much.

He didn't mention notifying a family member or a friend about his accident. Maybe he was married, but she hadn't seen any rings on his fingers. Of course that didn't necessarily mean anything. Some people couldn't wear rings or didn't choose to.

Though he spoke beautiful English, his name was French and she'd heard him mutter in French several times on the ride back to the museum from the river. Even in his dazed state, there was an undeniable sophistication about him that made him different from the other men she'd known in her life.

"He's what you call a gorgeous man, sweetheart." She spoke to the baby as she settled Elizabeth in the playpen with a noisy rattle to distract her. "I've seen them in films and magazines, so I know they exist. But I never met one in the flesh until last night. Whoever he is, I'm afraid I'll never forget him."

Up until the last Christmas recess, Hannah had been in graduate school at the University of Laramie where she'd dated various men on campus who'd seemed anxious to get to know her better. But over the holidays her younger sister Lisa had given birth to Elizabeth, and then had run away from home. She'd left no message where she was going or when she would be back.

In order to care for the baby who'd been virtually abandoned and needed her aunt desperately, Hannah's whole life had been turned around in a matter of hours. It meant putting her studies and social life on hold, but she wasn't complaining.

Compared to the welfare of a beautiful, innocent child, any sacrifice was worth it, especially when the baby was Hannah's flesh and blood. She would think about her own personal needs and desires at another time. Right now Elizabeth was her number-one priority.

After pressing a kiss to the baby's silken blond head, she hurriedly took advantage of the time to get the store part of the museum ready for business.

To her consternation, the stranger's image continued to haunt her all morning while she waited on customers. Finally, when Elizabeth went down for her afternoon nap and there was a lull in tourist activity, Hannah phoned the hospital for information.

She should have been relieved to learn that Mr. Giraud had already been discharged with nothing more than a headache and a sprained ankle. For his sake she *was* relieved.

What she couldn't understand was this unfathomable sense of disappointment that he'd already left the hospital. Not that she would ever have seen him again. Of course she wouldn't have. But it was just the idea that he'd come and gone so quickly from her life.

In ways, she wished the accident hadn't happened at all. She wished she'd never looked into the velvety-brown depths of his eyes, never felt the strength of his incredible physique, never held him close enough to breathe in his masculine scent, never touched his luxuriant hair, never memorized the strong lines of his darkly handsome features.

What a magnificent man...

The more she thought about him, the more she wondered what kind of business had brought a person like that out to Wyoming of all places. Even more puzzling, why had he been driving around on *her* property, especially when there was no road? None of it made sense.

At one point she chastised herself for allowing thoughts of him to impinge on her consciousness. All they did was remind her that for whatever reason he'd ventured into Wyoming territory, he probably wouldn't be staying here long. It was absurd to even entertain the hope of seeing him again or getting to know him better.

In fact she was so angry at her foolish, ridiculous imaginations, she intentionally exhausted her strength by spending the rest of the afternoon between customers unloading a week's work of saleable merchandise from the trunk of her car.

The latest stack of printed flyers needed to be scrolled and put out on the counter. They'd been made to look like authentic want ads. She tied each one with a thong to add the finishing touch. The flyers, along with the Pony Express Rider outfits and the colorful maps of the Pony Express Trail, were the items tourists always bought first. In fact they sold faster than anything else at the historic Sandhill way station museum.

It filled Hannah with pride that Sandhill stood on Carr property, one of the few stations across the country still remaining and still preserved in its original state since the 1860s.

Literally a crude log hut where the riders of old changed horses and bedded down for the night in a bunk, Hannah's deceased father, a rodeo champion turned postal worker who'd retired early due to a medical disability, had constructed a counter so they could turn the place into a shop as well as a museum.

Outside he'd restored the original makeshift barn. Hannah kept her mare there. Under her supervision parents paid good money to let their children have a ride around the small corral.

Thankful for the customers who flocked to Wyoming, especially during the summer months, Hannah counted on the revenue for her bread and butter. With Elizabeth to feed and clothe, back tuition fees to pay, plus the heavy expense of hiring a private detective to locate her missing sister, Hannah needed every dime she could save.

Two weeks ago she'd opened the museum to coincide with the end of classes at the university, the signal that summer had come to the state.

Now that the hotter weather had finally kicked in, the tourist season had started to pick up and would reach its peak through July and August. Tour bus groups spent the most money, especially the elderly couples.

While the men purchased maps and argued points of history, their wives thronged to the counter to buy Pony Express rider hats and trinkets for their grandchildren.

As soon as Hannah showed them the flyers, most of the women bought one, but so far Elizabeth had been the greatest attraction to date. The minute the women caught sight of the baby, everything stopped while they oohed and ahhed over her. Even the men couldn't resist patting her on the head. While everyone lingered, the sales continued to mount.

After this long Hannah had thought Elizabeth would have grown used to the attention, but she invariably burst into tears and would cling to Hannah, hiding her head so no one could get a good look at her. In fact she'd been fussy since the last busload pulled away.

The museum was no place for a baby. Mr. Moench, an attorney and old family friend who'd helped find a reputable private investigator to look for her sister had intimated as much, and no one knew it better than Hannah. The heat could be suffocating by the end of the day.

But even if she could have come up with the money for a woman to baby-sit Elizabeth at the claustrophobic apartment in Laramie, Hannah couldn't bear to be parted from her all day long. Her heart would have ached for the baby if they couldn't be together. Hannah loved Elizabeth every bit as much as if she'd given birth to her.

The baby was thriving and doing the most amazing things. She was a miracle. Hannah didn't want to miss a second of her development. Besides, Elizabeth needed her. She depended on her for literally everything... So there was no other choice but to make a difficult situation work, despite the obstacles.

Unfortunately after Hannah's last trip to the car, the baby seemed worse and refused to be comforted. Hannah had fed her and changed her diaper, but still her tears increased. Maybe she'd caught a cold and her tummy was sick.

"There, sweetheart. Don't cry," she crooned to her, reaching out a hand to feel her cheeks and forehead. In this heat Hannah couldn't tell if the two of them were just hot, or if the baby was running a temperature.

Growing more anxious, Hannah picked her up and started rocking her. When the baby cried harder, there was nothing to do but close the museum an hour early and take her to the nighttime pediatrics clinic in town. No matter how much she needed the money the store generated, Elizabeth's health came first.

She quickly placed the Closed sign in the window, then emptied the money box in an envelope, which she put in her purse. Grabbing the diaper bag she headed for the door with Elizabeth, only to be bombarded by another group of tourists making their way through the entry.

Hannah couldn't believe it. In her haste to get back to town, she hadn't heard another tour bus drive up. The confusion and noise upset the baby even more. She began crying at the top of her lungs.

On the verge of telling everyone they would have to leave because she was taking the baby to the doctor, she heard a deep, rich male voice say, *"Allow me."*

The next thing Hannah knew, a pair of bronzed, masculine hands came out of nowhere and plucked Elizabeth from her arms.

Caught off guard, Hannah spun around to find herself looking up at the breathtaking stranger from last night who seemed perfectly recovered after his accident.

He began whispering little French phrases to the baby that made Hannah's insides quiver for no reason. Slowly he started kissing Elizabeth's flushed cheeks.

At first the baby fussed, and though Hannah appreciated the stranger's attempts to help, she was ready to take Elizabeth back when by some miracle she started to quiet down.

Each kiss he bestowed silenced her a little more until a smile quivered on her rosebud mouth and she forgot to cry. Her moist, awestruck green eyes stared at his incredible masculine looks in rapt absorption.

Hannah had to suppress a moan. Even Elizabeth at her tender age had fallen under this man's powerful charisma and had become mesmerized by him. Within seconds she actually seemed content to be held close against his broad shoulder.

In absolute wonderment Hannah stood there and watched as the baby burrowed her face in his sun-tanned neck. That telling gesture not only meant Elizabeth felt secure, she craved the attention and comfort this man was willing to give her.

"Your husband certainly has a way with that adorable little girl of yours," one of the elderly female tourists said loud enough for everyone around to hear. But Hannah was so stunned by what she was seeing, she couldn't find the words to correct the woman's erroneous assumption.

The stranger's gaze found Hannah's once more. His intelligent dark brown eyes, fringed by even darker lashes, slowly traveled over her upturned features, reducing her limbs to water.

In a quiet aside he said, "This is the least I can do after your heroic gesture for me last night. Go ahead and finish waiting on your customers while this golden cherub and I get better acquainted. What do I call her?"

"E—" Hannah had to clear her throat. "Her name is Elizabeth."

CHAPTER TWO

"ELIZABETH." She heard him repeat the name in the French way before he kissed her tiny nose and cheeks once more.

The baby's mouth kept breaking into a smile. She was *loving* this! If she had a tummy ache, it didn't seem to be bothering her right now.

Hannah couldn't believe Elizabeth's reaction to the stranger. The baby had never let anyone else get this close to her except Hannah. For one ridiculous moment Hannah actually found herself envious of the infant who appeared to have captivated the man's attention so thoroughly.

He was so natural with her, Hannah imagined he must be a father several times over to know how to stop those tears. Of course a man like him would have a wife and family of his own, ring or no ring! It was ludicrous to believe anything else, let alone fantasize about him.

She quickly looked away and began waiting on the tourists lined up in front of the counter. For the next twenty minutes there was a steady stream of customers.

Every so often she stole a glance at the arresting stranger who moved back and forth with a slight limp while he rocked Elizabeth in his hard-muscled arms. Obviously content, the baby's eyelids had lowered to half-mast. So far not one peep had come out of her.

Judging by his demeanor, you would never have guessed he'd been semiconscious from a car accident last night.

Eventually the museum emptied. His gaze captured hers. "Are you going back to Laramie tonight?" There was a hint of compassion in his deep voice and eyes as he scrutinized Hannah's hot face.

She felt at such a disadvantage. Not since noon had she touched a brush to her curls or freshened her lipstick. With such intense heat she needed a shower and a change of clothes.

At one point Elizabeth had spit up. Part of it had come off on her blouse instead of the diaper she'd placed on her shoulder. Though she'd rinsed the material with some bottled water, she couldn't wait to get back to the apartment to start a wash.

"Yes."

"I am, too. When you're ready to close,

why don't you let me help by taking the baby out to your car while you lock up. Then I'll follow you into town. Perhaps after you've put her down for the night, we can talk.''

Her heart started to trip over itself. "Talk?"

"Yes. Yesterday I came out here for that very purpose, but you were busy. So I decided to ride around while I waited for that tour bus to leave. I'm afraid my concentration wasn't what it should be, and you know what happened.''

Hannah was very much afraid that she did. The incident had started up a curious ache that wasn't about to go away.

"But I'm not complaining," he murmured in a husky voice. "Last night I found out for myself there really are golden-haired angels.'' His intent gaze traveled down the length of her curvaceous body, filling her with a different kind of heat. "I just didn't know they came to earth wearing cowboy boots.''

Hannah swallowed hard at that sensual perusal. "Perhaps it would be better if you stated your business now, Mr. Giraud.''

"The name is Dominic. And yours?" he inquired mildly.

"I—it's Hannah," she stammered. "Hannah Carr.''

She hadn't meant to sound so defensive just now, but it was the only way she knew how to deal with her chaotic emotions. While he stood this close to her, she was too confused to think straight.

Hannah couldn't take much more of this or she would lose any objectivity she had left. "If you don't mind my asking, why did you bother driving all the way out here again?"

"To thank you properly for saving my life." He reached in his back pocket. The next thing she knew he'd placed a five-hundred-dollar bill on the counter next to the infant seat.

She didn't make a move to pick it up. "I didn't save your life, Mr. Giraud, and I would never take your money."

"Please allow me to repay you in some small way. Spend it on this precious baby if you won't use it for yourself. You played the good Samaritan, and I'm very grateful."

Hannah shook her head. "Are you aware I might have done real damage by removing you from the accident site without knowing if you had a broken neck or spine or some such thing?"

His penetrating eyes narrowed on her classic features. 'The memories are somewhat vague, but I do recall insisting on getting to my feet. You couldn't stop me. Which means I didn't leave you with any other choice than to assist me. Let's be clear about that, shall we?''

His voice had taken on an edge that held more than a trace of steel. For a brief moment she had the strongest suspicion he was an intimidating, powerful force among his peers.

Some men were natural-born leaders who lit their own fires. He was that kind of man, and all the more intriguing because of his unfeigned display of loving tenderness with the baby.

Some of Hannah's male neighbors and friends had been around Elizabeth enough times for her to recognize them and respond. But she always shied away from any attention they tried to give her.

"If you're still insistent about not taking my money, will you at least allow me to buy you dinner tomorrow night to show my gratitude? That invitation includes your husband and Elizabeth, of course."

She sucked in her breath. "There's no husband. It's just the baby and me." *Until Lisa comes back on her own, or is found. Please, God, let her be safe. Let her return home soon.*

Upon that admission, his dark gaze collided with hers. "I'm staying at the Executive Inn in Laramie. If you'll tell me where you live," he said in a silken voice, "I'll pick you up at seven."

"It really isn't necessary, Mr. Giraud."

"The name is Dominic," he affirmed forcefully, "and I beg to differ with you. Without your help the other night, I might have stumbled into the river and lost consciousness."

As she shuddered at the very idea of such a ghastly scenario, she felt him watching her.

"Do we have a date?" he prodded. Hannah had the impression this man wouldn't give up until she'd accepted his invitation. "I'll let you decide where we eat. Over our meal I'll tell you the reason why I was driving behind the museum in the first place."

Her pulse raced.

The idea of going anywhere with him, let alone to dinner, filled her with too much excitement. She had to remember that he could be a married man, and that he wasn't asking her out for romantic reasons.

Because she wouldn't take his money, this was the only other way he could think of to pay her back for getting him to a hospital. To read anything else into his invitation was ridiculous, especially when he'd suggested that her husband join them.

What she needed to do was treat this like she would any business dinner. Moistening her lips nervously she said, "The Executive Inn has a good restaurant. Why don't I meet you there at seven-thirty? If Elizabeth cooperates, we should be on time."

His veiled eyes played over her face. "I'll wait as long as it takes."

For no good reason her heart took up its crazy pounding again.

"I believe you've got customers."

Hannah jerked her head toward the door, hoping to hide the blush that started at her toes and quickly enveloped her entire body, including her face. She should have been the one to notice what was going on at her own establishment!

"Before I leave, why don't I put Elizabeth in her playpen and make certain she stays asleep before I go. How does that sound?"

It sounded heavenly, *too* heavenly.

She darted him a quick glance once more. "Much as I appreciate your offer, surely you have other pressing business."

One dark brow dipped ominously as a string of tourists filed into the museum. "I thought by now you understood that *you're* my pressing business,'' he muttered, staring hard at her before he moved behind the counter with the baby.

While Hannah waited on customers, she glanced repeatedly in his direction, unable to resist watching the gentle way he treated Elizabeth. Something told Hannah that if she wasn't careful, Dominic Giraud had the power to infiltrate her mind and heart until she didn't know herself anymore.

Long after he'd left the museum, she was still haunted by the private message his eyes had conveyed before he'd walked out the door.

Maybe it was a trick of light in the museum, but for a brief moment his regard had seemed intimate. She gasped softly just remembering it, then regretted her foolish behavior when the customer she was waiting on asked her if she was all right.

Embarrassed, Hannah assured the woman she was fine. But of course she wasn't fine at all. She was a jumbled mass of nerves and anticipation all rolled together. There'd be no sleep for her tonight!

In a testy mood, which was rare for him, Dominic limped out to his rental car and headed for town, missing his Jeep that was still being repaired and wouldn't be ready for pick up until tomorrow.

To his recollection no female of his acquaintance had ever refused a gift from him before, monetary or otherwise. If he were really being honest with himself, no woman had ever been as resistant to his attention.

On the contrary, of the limited number of relationships he'd had since his twenties, he'd always been the one to walk away first, unable to commit.

What surprised him was how much it rankled to *have* to talk Ms. Carr into joining him for dinner. He wondered if she was still emotionally involved with the baby's father. The possibility that she might have a new lover and intended to spend the night in his bed sounded equally distasteful to Dominic.

However, a lover he could deal with. A husband was something else. He gritted his teeth, unconsciously gunning the accelerator at the same time as he drove away.

Though his father held to no such code of ethics, married women had always been off limits to Dominic. Furthermore, unlike his womanizing parent whose infidelity had caused incalculable grief to Dominic's mother, marriage had never figured in Dominic's plans.

Just remembering the past caused a blackness to envelop him. Not wanting to go down that treacherous path tonight, he reached for his cell phone to call Zane.

"Salut—" he said as soon as his friend answered.

"Dom! How are things progressing?"

"I'm not sure," he muttered before he realized how revealing the comment sounded.

"What's that supposed to mean? You've run into snags before, but they've never bothered you."

Dominic rubbed the side of his jaw absently. He wouldn't exactly describe Hannah Carr as a snag.

After a pause, "What's going on?"

He sucked in his breath. "I wish I knew."

"You're being cryptic, buddy, and that's making me edgy."

"You've hit on the right word."

"So, how long are you going to keep me in the dark?"

"I'm pulling into my hotel now. Give me a minute to get up to my room and then I'll call you back and tell you about my accident."

Another silence. "Were you hurt?"

He shut off the motor. "It could have been worse if this angel hadn't saved me."

"*Angel?* What on earth are you talking about? Dom?"

Elizabeth woke up hungry from her afternoon nap. Since there was a lull between customers, Hannah decided to call it a day and close up shop early. She could no longer function with any coherence.

After putting Cinnamon in the barn, and making sure the mare had enough water along with her oats, they headed for home. There were a dozen things to be done and little time to accomplish everything before they left for the hotel.

Once inside the apartment, she fed the baby, gave her a bath, then put her in a playpen in the bedroom. That freed up Hannah's time so she could shower and wash her own hair.

It felt good to get clean and put on fresh underwear. The problem was finding something suitable to wear. She had no intention of dressing up for Mr. Giraud, but naturally she wouldn't wear trousers.

Hannah possessed several nice winter outfits to wear at university functions. What she needed was a new summer wardrobe, but she couldn't afford one.

That meant she would have to settle for her

sundress. It was a sleeveless pale yellow cotton with a modest neckline, always in style. She could wear her white sandals and a single strand of pearls.

After she'd dressed and fixed herself a lemonade, she phoned Bob Arnold, the P.I. working on Lisa's case. To her chagrin he told her the same thing he'd been telling her for months.

He still hadn't found Lisa, but Hannah wasn't to give up. Often these situations took a long time.

Hannah told him she understood, but it was hard to wait. Every day Lisa was gone put more emotional distance between mother and daughter. As for the financial side of it, Hannah's money was running out, but she kept that news to herself. It was vital that Lisa be found no matter how much it cost!

With a mixture of aching sadness and anxiety over her sister, Hannah checked herself in the mirror one more time. The worry, combined with several sleeplessness nights had put hollows beneath her eyes. They looked more like smudges.

If she wore thick makeup, she could probably cover them up, but Hannah had never put anything on her skin except lotion.

After their mother had died giving birth to

Lisa, their father turned into a very strict parent. As both girls matured, he forbade them to use anything artificial.

"You have been given golden hair, green eyes and a peaches-and-cream complexion like your mother's. You need no other embellishment, so let that be the end of it."

Probably because Hannah had been the elder sister by eight years, she'd obeyed him without question. Lisa, on the other hand, fought his unyielding authority every step of the way. Their fights had always upset Hannah.

She would slip out the back door and ride her horse until she was sure their latest quarrel was over. Then she would go back to the house where inevitably she would find her sister in the bedroom crying.

The pattern continued until their father died. At that point Hannah tried to keep their little household going and oversee their meager finances, but Lisa loved the freedom and became more defiant than ever.

Now she was gone, and Hannah began to wonder if she would ever come home. Swallowing the lump in her throat, she dashed to the closet for the baby stroller. After she put it in the car, she hurried back inside the apartment for Elizabeth.

Unable to resist, she leaned down to kiss her pink cheeks. "Right now it's just the two of us. Thank heaven for you," she whispered emotionally, then straightened.

"Now, are you ready to have dinner with Mr. Giraud? We really shouldn't, you know. He's an experienced man of the world. Far too sophisticated and fascinating for us to handle, so don't get too attached to him, sweetheart. After tonight we may never see him again."

It was good advice.

Too bad Hannah's heart hadn't heeded the warning when she'd first seen him lying in the grass.

Just the anticipation of being with him again made her breathing shallow. To her alarm, by the time they reached the hotel parking lot, her cheeks were flushed even though she'd been running the air conditioner at full strength.

"Oh!" she cried when her door was opened for her and she saw him standing there in a pearl-gray summer suit and white shirt. He'd been waiting for them.

His appeal overwhelmed her.

"Good evening, Hannah. You're right on time." Their eyes met before hers looked away in confusion, but she could feel his frank leisurely appraisal. It missed nothing.

She felt his hand on her bare upper arm assisting her out of the car. His touch sent a river of warmth through her body.

"I'll get Elizabeth."

Before she could gather her wits, he'd relinquished his hold of her to open the back door and lift the baby from the car seat.

"Hmm, *mignonne*. You smell as sweet as you look," he murmured into her neck, then kissed her on her cheeks and chin. Elizabeth laughed out loud.

Hannah could see her advice had been wasted on the baby. They were both in deep water as far as this man was concerned.

Thinking of his immaculate suit, Hannah lifted a clean cloth to Dominic's shoulder in case the baby spit up. She had to rise on tiptoe and it brought her head close to his. Inadvertently her fingers grazed his strong jawline,

"Here, you better have this, Mr. Giraud," she said nervously.

This time his eyes, dark and unexpectedly fierce, trapped hers. "Why do you find it so impossible to call me Dominic?"

Shaken by his intensity, she backed away from him with a jerky movement. "Probably because I was raised to be formal around people just passing through.''

His brows knit together in a frown. ''I'm afraid I did a lot more than simply pass through. I *trespassed* on your property, forcing you to leave Elizabeth alone to rescue me from a precarious situation. You had no idea who or what you'd find when you got out there.

''The Jeep could have exploded into flames, but that didn't deter you. Most people wouldn't have known how to handle the situation, let alone been ingenious enough to put me on a horse and get me to safety. You held me so I wouldn't fall,'' he added in husky tone. ''That night we became more than strangers, Hannah.''

There was a trace of accent when he said her name. She loved the way it sounded on his lips.

Breaking free of his piercing glance, Hannah went to get the stroller.

''From the way Elizabeth is behaving, it appears she agrees with you,'' she observed in a wry tone to cover her chaotic emotions.

Without waiting for his response, she began walking toward the restaurant entrance of the inn and pushed the stroller in front of her. He adjusted his stride to keep pace, his limp barely noticeable. As they entered the foyer, a couple of girls around nine or ten standing with their parents at the checkout counter caught a glimpse of Elizabeth and skipped over to Dominic. The one in glasses looked straight up at him. "Your baby girl is so cute!"

"I think she is, too," he said with all the tenderness of a proud, new father.

His answer, especially the way he said it, caught Hannah unaware. She found herself swallowing hard.

"Will you let us look at her?" the other one piped up.

He flashed them a smile that took Hannah's breath. "Elizabeth is a little shy around strangers, so don't feel bad if she starts to cry."

In a deft move he turned the baby and lowered her to their eye level. On cue, her lower lip quivered. Within seconds her face screwed up and she burst into tears.

"You just want your daddy, huh." While one tickled her chin, the other tried to grasp her tiny fingers.

Hannah fought the instinct to reach for the baby. If anyone tried to take her from Dominic right now, Elizabeth wouldn't stand for it. As it was, she was already creating a fuss. Heads turned in their direction.

By the glint in his eye, Dominic found it all very amusing as he put the baby back in her favorite place against his heart. Content once more, she quieted down.

The girls thanked him and ran over to their parents.

He darted Hannah an amused glance. "Shall we go in?"

She took a deep breath. "I'm not sure if Elizabeth will hold out through a long meal. Perhaps it would be better if we put her back in the car and went to a drive-in. LaRue's at the other end of town makes good homemade hamburgers." Hannah was suddenly sure that sharing an expensive meal with this compelling man wasn't a good idea.

"That's hardly what I had in mind for tonight."

"I realize that, but a baby has a way of changing the best-laid plans." After a hesitation, "I'll remember the thought, Dominic," she added quietly.

"Will you?" he murmured, his gaze suddenly inscrutable. All mirth had vanished, making her the slightest bit uneasy.

She hoped he couldn't tell her hands were trembling as she opened her purse. "Here are my keys if you'd like to drive. Oh, and here's that five-hundred-dollar bill. You forgot to take it with you.''

As Dominic pulled to a stop at the drive-in, he decided the change in plans suited his purposes much better. Eating together in the small confines of her car kept things more intimate. Best of all, the baby seemed content in her infant seat. As long as she was being good, her mother couldn't use her as a shield to avoid concentrating on him.

He'd never had Hannah Carr's undivided attention except at the accident scene when he'd only been semiconscious. *Things were about to change.*

A middle-aged woman walked up to them and put a card under the windshield wiper. ''Hi! What can I get for you?''

While he gave the waitress their order, he could feel her unsolicited scrutiny.

''Excuse me, but haven't I seen you before?''

Throughout his life this sort of inquisition had happened so constantly, he'd been forced to learn to live with it. But tonight the intrusion on his privacy made him angry.

''I'm afraid not.''

''But I *have.* I saw you on TV.''

"I probably resemble someone you saw," he muttered. *So much for anonymity here.* The fates continued to conspire against him and his desire to be alone with Hannah.

"No. You were on the *America Today* show, but you're even more handsome in person. I told my husband you have a French name. I remember it because I love the sound of it. Dominic."

He winced.

"I'm sorry if I've embarrassed you, but this is so exciting. The two men on the program with you were good-looking, too. I have to tell you—that was the most fascinating program I've seen in years!"

"Is that right?"

"Absolutely! I hope this means you're running your bullet train through Laramie. I've got a husband who won't get on an airplane, and hates long drives in the car. When that thing is built, we can go anywhere we want in a hurry and never leave the ground. Just like that!" She snapped her fingers.

"After I bring your food, can I have your autograph? Unless I show proof, my husband won't believe you really came to LaRue's to eat with your family. That's a little doll you've got back there. She's going to grow up to be a real heartbreaker just like her daddy, I bet.''

While he attempted to suppress a groan, he felt Hannah lean across him to talk to the waitress.

"If you'll bring back a menu with our food, I'll make sure Dominic signs it. What's your name?''

Her eyes lit up. "Marie. Marie Gates. Thank you. Thank you so much! Since you're his wife, I want *you* to sign it, too. All right?''

"She'll do it,'' Dominic assured the woman with relish before his gaze shifted to a pair of eyes whose impossibly green color rivaled the grass he'd seen growing in an Oregonian rainforest. The combination of dark lashes and delicately shaped eyebrows beneath those natural golden curls highlighted their beauty.

Every perfect feature of her oval face, particularly her sculpted lips, a larger version of Elizabeth's, drew his attention so he didn't want to look anywhere else. He'd never known a woman who had such a seductive mouth and flawless complexion. It would be as soft and silky as the baby's.

Except for lipstick, she wore no makeup. Nature had blessed her with creamy skin that millions of women spent billions of dollars on cosmetics to replicate. Dominic knew this to be true more than any man. Those billions made up his family's vast fortune. He bet if he looked in her purse or bathroom, he wouldn't find *one* House of Eve product anywhere. What an irony.

With such a face and voluptuous curves, how on earth could any man have walked away from her and Elizabeth?

Was she still in love with him?

It made no sense to Dominic *unless* she was a widow. If that was the case, it might explain the faint shadows beneath her eyes.

He let go of the breath he'd been holding. So many questions needed answers, but he would have to proceed slowly.

"You shouldn't have told the waitress I would give her an autograph, Dominic," she said at last.

His lips twitched. "What's sauce for the gander..."

"May be, but this goose doesn't happen to be your wife."

"Since I'm not married and never have been, I don't see the problem. Don't you know there's an old adage that white lies are the good kind?"

"You made that up."

He chuckled. "Even if I did, it's true. Think how happy it will make her."

"Uh-oh. She's coming with our food."

"*Dieu merci!* I'm ravenous."

"Here you go." The waitress fastened the tray of food to the lowered glass of the car window.

"How much do I owe you?"

"Since you're going to autograph this for me, not one cent." She handed him a new menu and pen through the opening.

He signed it, then gave everything back along with a twenty-dollar bill.

"'Dear Marie.'" She read the words aloud. "'We hope you and your husband enjoy many train rides across the country in the near future. With sincerest regards, Mr. and Mrs. Dominic Giraud.'"

Her head lifted. "Oh, my. This is wonderful. But I can't take the money."

"I insist."

"Well, thank you again."

"You're welcome."

"When you're through, just blink your lights and I'll come for the tray."

As she hurried off, Dominic turned to his

lovely companion who'd remained silent during the exchange. He put a straw in her drink and handed her what she'd ordered.

"Alone at last."

CHAPTER THREE

CHAPTER THREE

HANNAH took the food from him, trying her hardest not to let the news that he was a bachelor affect her.

It certainly couldn't have been for lack of opportunity that he hadn't married. Maybe he'd buried his heart with someone he'd loved, and since then had thrown himself into his career.

"I'm afraid I missed that program on TV Marie was referring to. What is it exactly that you do for a living, Dominic?" She'd been dying of curiosity.

He stared at her over the rim of his root beer mug. "I travel across the country convincing landowners like you to become part of an exciting transportation idea for the twenty-first century."

But that didn't pay his bills for food, gas, hotels, the repairs to his damaged Jeep. The five hundred dollars he'd tried to give her had to come from somewhere!

"Let me ask you a question," he said

softly. "Who owns the property the museum stands on?"

His question came as a surprise. "It's been in my family for generations."

Something flickered in the dark recesses of his unforgettable brown eyes fringed with an overabundance of black lashes. Once again she was struck by the male beauty of this fascinating man.

"Whom would I speak to about using your land for a project I'm involved in?"

"You mean the bullet train Marie was referring to a moment ago?"

"That's right. I'd like permission to run train track across your property."

"You're really going to build one?"

His mouth twitched provocatively. "Your incredulity doesn't surprise me. Everyone I've spoken to has had the same initial reaction. I represent a group of people dedicated to building a special train which will stretch from New York to San Francisco."

"You mean like the kind in Japan?"

"Exactly. It will operate on the principle of magnetic levitation, but this one will run close to five hundred miles per hour. Naturally before such an enterprise can get off the ground, permission must be obtained by everyone who owns land where the proposed track will be forged. Your property lies along the route we've already surveyed by air."

At last she had the reason for his presence on her land the other night.

"Both owners on either side of you have given us the go-ahead."

The unexpected news threw her. She shook her head in disbelief. "They're selling their land to you?"

Her question caused the baby to stir in the back seat. Any second now and pandemonium could reign once more.

"No. We're not asking anyone to sell anything, except as a last resort of course. We prefer offering stock in our company for the use of the land. One day in the future the dividends will be worth a great deal of money."

Hannah faced him directly. "It's an incredible concept, and I can't help but admire the vision of such a project. I've heard the French have them, too. But even if you should make that dream a reality here in the States, I'm afraid I can't give you the permission you're looking for.

"Though it's a very exciting idea running a bullet train through here, you have to understand the land is an historical site which my family has kept intact over generations. I could never sell it or allow it to be tampered with. I'm sorry,'' she added lamely because she really would have liked to have told him yes.

After another bite of her hamburger she said, ''It sounds like an impossible feat, but I don't suppose that word is in your vocabulary.''

''You're right.'' His slow smile played havoc with her emotions. There was still so much she sensed he hadn't told her.

''I couldn't be the only person who has turned you down.''

''No.''

Unable to meet his steady gaze, she looked back at Elizabeth who'd fallen asleep again. ''What do you do when that happens?''

''I hope they'll change their minds. Since I conceived my dream, ninety-nine percent of the landowners I've talked to need a few days or weeks before they come around to the idea. It usually takes that long for them to catch the vision. Once they do, the paperwork can begin. In the meantime I look for alternative routes.''

''But that must be so frustrating!''

''At times it is, especially when dealing with state and federal government officials.

But no dream worth its salt comes without disappointments and setbacks.''

"I can't imagine such a gargantuan project. Won't it take you months just to procure all the rights?''

"It already has, and I've only reached the eastern sector of Wyoming. That still leaves the western half, Utah, Nevada and California. But there's plenty of time and I'm in no hurry.'' He finished off the rest of his hamburger.

She flicked at an imaginary piece of lint on her thigh. 'Hypothetically speaking, tell me why I would want the train to run across my land, aside from the stock options.''

"Perhaps for you personally, I can't provide a reason. But you heard Marie. Her husband won't fly. There are millions of people who have that same fear, yet they want to travel the vast expanse of this continent. A car is too slow, too dangerous and too confining.

"The train rides on a cushion of air at tremendous speed without harming the environment. An engineer who happens to be a close personal friend and colleague of mine, has produced a prototype which runs quietly, safely and allows the passenger to see the country at the same time.

"But such a train will never exist unless thousands of people and governmental agencies are willing to share their property for the common good."

She shook her head. "It isn't that I'm not willing to share my land, but before my father died, he made me promise that I would hold on to it and never alter it."

There's another reason. It's Lisa's land, too, and she's not here to give her permission.

"A promise should be kept. Don't worry. I'll solve my problem. I always do."

He was being very gracious about it, but she'd felt his underlying passion for the project.

"This whole idea is your brainchild, isn't it?"

Quiet reigned until she heard him clear his throat. "That's right."

Perhaps her curiosity was irritating him, but she couldn't seem to stop asking questions. This man had many facets to his character. She yearned to explore them all.

"Are *you* afraid of flying?" she asked gently. "Is that what promp—"

"The answer is no," he broke in on her before she could finish. "But my English-born mother goes into shock at the very thought of getting on a ship or a plane.

"When I moved to New York, she used to tell me she would give anything in the world if a train could be built across the ocean so she could come and stay with me in New York when she liked. Though I couldn't grant her that wish, it got me thinking."

The bits and pieces of information he tossed her way were pure torture because she sensed there was so much more he wasn't telling her.

Some people dreamed dreams. But you didn't dream his kind of dream unless you rubbed shoulders with other visionaries. People who knew the right kind of people in order to undertake a project of herculean proportions. She'd been right all along in thinking Dominic Giraud was no ordinary man.

More than ever she could understand why he hadn't acquired a wife. It would take a special woman to challenge his mind, let alone capture his heart.

Aware that the ache in hers had grown acute, Hannah realized it was long past time to go home to her world.

"That's a very touching story." No doubt the slight wobble in her voice gave away the state of her emotions. "I'm sure your mother must be thrilled that you're making her wish a reality somewhere else in the world, even if she can't enjoy it. Now, if you don't mind, I think we'd better go. Elizabeth and I have to be up early in the morning.''

"So do I.'' His voice grated.

He was leaving.

She'd known it was likely. The thought of his not being here anymore filled her with an emptiness, that frightened and surprised her.

Quickly she handed him the cup and wrapper to put back on the tray. He flashed his lights and Marie hurried over to them.

"How was your meal?''

"That was the best hamburger I've ever tasted.''

She beamed. "I'll tell the owner. Don't be a stranger now,'' she called over her shoulder.

Hannah's eyes closed tightly. She could have echoed those words.

Too disturbed by the trend of her thoughts, she couldn't bring herself to make desultory conversation. Rather, she pretended interest out of her side window until they reached the hotel.

Instead of pulling up to the lobby entrance, he drove around the back and stopped behind his Jeep. Before she could blink he'd levered himself from the driver's seat and had come around to open her door.

"Thank you," she whispered. His close proximity forced her to brush against him before she could move around to get behind the wheel of the car. At this point her whole body was reacting to that brief pleasurable contact, and she had difficulty turning on the engine.

"The dinner was very enjoyable. Thank you. G-good luck to you, Dominic," she stammered because he wasn't saying anything. "I really do wish you great success with your project."

His eyes narrowed on her upturned features. "Why don't we save our goodbyes until I've seen you safely home."

Her heart thudded. *He meant to follow her in his Jeep.*

By the time they'd reached the parking space at the side of the fourplex, she'd become a trembling mass of emotions. No sooner had she turned off the motor than he'd reached inside to pull Elizabeth from her car seat.

Hannah raced up the outside steps to the second level. With the keys already in her hand, she shouldn't have had any problem with the lock to her apartment. But for some reason, the front door key refused to fit all the way. The next thing she knew Dominic's hand reached in to help, and *voilà*. They both heard the click.

Fighting for composure she said, "Thank you for all your help. I can manage now." She turned to take the baby, but he'd already opened the door and had slipped past her into the living room where she'd left a lamp light on.

Once they were inside she reached for Elizabeth who began to cry at being so cruelly plucked from those masculine arms.

Hugging the baby to her she said, "Thank you for seeing us home. Now I think you'd better go. As long as Elizabeth knows you're here, she'll be impossible."

"I'm leaving," he muttered, "but I'll be back. Goodnight."

She thought he meant to kiss the baby's cheek, but it was Hannah's mouth he brushed with his own before disappearing out the door.

His touch set off sensations through her body not unlike a current of electricity.

"I know exactly how you feel," she whispered to a seemingly inconsolable Elizabeth as they headed for the nursery. "But he said he'd be back."

She'd learned enough about him to know

he meant what he said. She also knew he was a busy man with tremendous responsibilities. It might be weeks before he could fit in another visit to Laramie.

Realizing the wait was going to feel like an eternity, Hannah made up her mind to stay so busy she wouldn't have time to think about how meeting him had transformed her life.

But after a whole week and no word from him, she began to think the connection she'd been sure was between them was all in her imagination. If his feelings had been as strong as hers, he would have found a way to see her again, even if it had only been for an hour.

She'd gone out to the museum every day as early as possible, and had stayed later than usual on the chance that he would drop by. The fact that he hadn't made one appearance there, or at the apartment, dashed any hopes she'd entertained of his falling in love with her.

A man in his mid-thirties who'd eluded marriage this long wasn't interested in commitment, especially a man with a mission like Dominic. Since Hannah wasn't interested in anything but the ultimate commitment of marriage, the whole situation was ludicrous, anyway.

Though Friday was one of her most lucrative days at the museum, there was no way she could stand to put herself through more purgatory hoping he would show up, only to have that dream shattered.

Instead, she gave the apartment a good cleaning, then dropped off the baby at her friend Elaine's so she could get her car safety inspected. While she waited in the lounge of Thornton's Garage, she thumbed through the only two magazines on the table. Nothing held her interest.

When the customer before her was told his car was ready, he tossed the magazine he'd been reading on the table. For want of anything else to do, she picked it up, hoping to put Dominic out of her mind, if only for a few minutes.

Seeing it was a back issue of *U.S. Economics,* required reading for one of her classes last Fall, she picked it up. The front page blurb captured her interest, as it was meant to do. She turned to the feature article about America's billionaires who now numbered two hundred and eighty-nine.

She couldn't imagine one person being worth that much money. Neither could the rest of the world, which was probably why the article made such fascinating copy, even to Hannah.

Page after page she scanned the pictures of ordinary-looking men and women throughout the globe with extraordinary monetary assets.

"Hannah? Your car's ready."

"Thanks, Jim. I'll be right there," she called back to him, ready to put the magazine down until she saw an unforgettable face that made her cry out in disbelief.

Dominic! She lurched in her chair and clutched the magazine more tightly.

There were two pictures of him. The first one showed him entering an office building from a busy street, dressed in an impeccable dark business suit and tie. He didn't look happy to be caught on film.

"'Dominic Giraud, the handsome, sought-after bachelor CEO of Giraud's House of Eve located in Provence, France, outside his American headquarters in New York City. Estimated assets: 70 billion.'"

Hannah gasped. The *House of Eve* was his family's business? She was incredulous. The reknowned French cosmetics company was a household name throughout the world. One Christmas Hannah had bought her father one of their men's colognes, a lime scent she particularly loved.

The second picture showed him pulling away from the gates of his ancestral villa in St. Paul de Vence, driving a sleek black luxury car, the expression on his devastatingly handsome face unsmiling and remote.

A picture said many things.

This picture whispered of a lifetime of exclusivity.

In one glance Hannah felt the enormous gap between them. In Dominic's case, it was more like the Grand Canyon, a natural wonder you couldn't bridge.

Without taking a breath she gazed at the pictures for endless minutes. Like pure revelation, all the pieces of the mystifying puzzle Dominic had presented, fit into place, like the waitress's insistence that she'd seen him interviewed about his project on national television. Each snippet of conversation suddenly made perfect sense. Hannah now had answers to those niggling questions she hadn't dared ask him about his family. Except for one...

What do you do for a living, Mr. Giraud?

I travel around the country talking to landowners like you.

She buried her face in her hands. A man like him could have anything he wanted— Whatever he wanted— *Whoever* he wanted.

Well it certainly wouldn't be you, Hannah Carr.

You knew the other night this was all too good to be true. You knew it, but you didn't want to believe it. You've been in denial because you wanted something you couldn't have.

You're not in his league.

Maybe no woman was. Maybe that was why he had never married.

He's certainly not going to take you home to meet the family. He hasn't even told you about them. He hasn't breathed one word about who he really is because he doesn't consider it necessary. You were a temporary diversion. That's all!

There were probably countless other women who'd been in the same position as Hannah, aching for anything he would give them until he grew bored of their company.

If you ever needed a way to get over Dominic Giraud, this article has just provided you the means.

Hannah jumped out of the chair and hurried to the office to pay her bill.

"Jim?" she asked after he'd given her the key and her papers. "Could I have this magazine? It's over a year old. There's an important article I want to keep. Do you mind? I'll pay you for it.''

"You're one of my favorite customers. Go on and take it.'' He cocked his head. "I see you don't have the little princess with you today."

"It's a rare sight, isn't it?" she quipped to cover her anguish. "Thanks for everything, Jim." She hurried out to the lot for her car, praying she would make it before anyone saw the tears gush down her cheeks.

She'd gleaned enough from being around Dominic to know he was a highly educated man of sophistication and experience, far removed from her world. But even *her* active imagination couldn't have thought up what she'd read just now.

The magazine would serve as her reality check. In future, whenever she found herself in danger of wanting what she couldn't have, she would open it to the article and take a good look at his pictures.

A few minutes later Hannah had picked up the baby from Elaine's and driven back to the apartment. Once there, she paced the floor with Elizabeth. Finally she couldn't stand it any longer.

"Let's go to the park. You'd like that, wouldn't you, sweetheart? We'll find a shady tree by the brook where you can watch butterflies, and I can mend the shirt I need to wear in next week's parade with the brigade and..." But she couldn't talk anymore because she'd burst into tears.

Dominic and Zane waved to Alik from the Jeep. He flashed them a grin as he strode toward them from the Cessna that had flown him into Laramie. In seconds he'd levered himself into the back seat with his duffel bag and briefcase.

"Glad you could make it, *mon vieux*."

"I'm relieved you moved the meeting up. This is one break I've needed despite the fact that there's a lot we have to discuss."

"I agree. This seemed as good a time as any to get together and see where we are, make a few projections."

"So, what's this Zane told me about your bachelor status about to go up in smoke?"

"You said that?" Dominic demanded of Zane as they drove toward the highway.

His friend broke out in a benign smile.

Alik clasped his shoulder from behind. "How soon is the wedding?"

"I have no idea."

"You want our approval first, is that it?"

"It's Ms. Carr's approval I'm worried

about,'' Dominic muttered. ''For some reason I have yet to discover, she is determined that there will be no 'us.'''

The guys chuckled.

''I didn't think there was a woman in existence who would ever give you a hard time,'' Alik mocked.

''You haven't met Hannah.''

Zane put on his sunglasses against the glare of the midafternoon sun. ''If Dom can't bring her around, then it can't be done.''

''When are we going to meet this *femme fatale?*''

''In about five minutes.''

Dominic had been living for it. After one long week of deprivation, he couldn't take any more. The sexual tension between them had been so strong, he was convinced her ex-lover couldn't have a hold on her.

Something else was preventing Hannah from responding to him. He knew in his gut she wanted him as much as he wanted her. *Mon Dieu!* He'd never felt like this before in his life. It had taken every atom of self-control not to make love to her, but after a week he'd come to a point of no return where she was concerned.

''We want to see where you rolled the Jeep.''

"How did you let a thing like that happen?" Alik mocked.

"I have a theory," Zane interjected before Dominic could get a word in edgewise. "It was fate, considering he was rescued by an angel."

"In cowboy boots, I understand. Dom— don't look now but there's a highway patrol car on the other side of the median. He's turning around. You'd better slow down."

"It's all right," Dominic muttered "Here's the turnoff to Hannah's place. I doubt he'll bother to follow us."

Another couple of miles and her property came into view. His gaze took in the corral. There was no sign of her horse. When he drew up in front of the museum, the Closed sign in the window had the effect of a well-placed kick in the gut.

He knew how much Hannah needed the money. If she wasn't here, it was because either she or the baby was ill. A nerve started to hammer at his temples.

The guys remained silent.

"I'll drive you out to the ridge before we head to town."

Revving the engine, he made a sharp turn to the right, kicking up dust as he drove past the museum.

*   *   *

Hannah didn't return to the apartment until dinnertime. Once she'd bathed the baby, she put her in her crib.

After starting a meal for herself, she listened to her answering machine, anxious to find out if the P.I. had called her. There was no message. While trying to recover from that disappointment, the doorbell rang.

She was in no mood to see or talk to anyone, but it was probably a neighbor who'd seen her come home and needed something.

Walking through to the living room she called out, "Who is it?"

"Dominic."

Dominic! He *had* come back.

With trembling hands she opened the door. There he stood in a navy silk shirt and tan chinos while she was still in the blouse and jeans she'd worn to the park. He looked magnificent.

She felt like she was going to faint from excitement, but he seemed oblivious as he scrutinized her face and body with haunting thoroughness. Nervously she smoothed an errant golden curl from her forehead.

"You look flushed," he said without preamble, his gaze never leaving her face. "Have you been ill? Is that why you didn't go out to the museum today?"

"No— I'm fine." It was a lie.

"What about Elizabeth?"

"She's fine, too."

"May I come in?"

Now that she had her heart's desire, she couldn't think. "Yes. Of course. Forgive me."

She opened the door wider, noticing he was carrying a shopping bag in one hand as he moved past her. Their bodies brushed ever so slightly, sending fire through hers.

His tall masculine frame dwarfed the small front room like before. Thank heaven she'd cleaned house this morning. With such a small apartment holding a lifetime of furnishings plus most of the baby's things and all her schoolbooks, the interior looked cluttered at any time. But at least there were no messes and the carpet had been vacuumed.

He set the bag down, then moved to a side table where Hannah kept some little framed pictures of the family. Just as she was hoping he wouldn't ask any questions, he said, "Who's this?"

"That's my sister, Lisa."

"She looks a lot like you. How old is she?"

"Eighteen now." She'd had a birthday two months ago, one they hadn't celebrated.

Another painful day to get through. "I know this room is hot, even with the fan on. Would you like something to drink?" Hannah was desperate to change the subject.

"No, thank you." He turned around, studying her intently with his dark, level gaze. "I came over here to ask you out to dinner. My friends Alik and Zane are in town. If you can't find a sitter, they could perhaps tend Elizabeth, I can vouch for their trustworthiness."

"Are these friends the ones involved in your project?" She'd asked the question to give herself time to assimilate the fact that he wanted to take her out tonight. But now that she'd read about him in that magazine, everything had changed.

"That's right. We needed a meeting, so I asked them to fly into Laramie. Naturally they heard about my accident and wanted to visit the scene of the crime. I brought them to the museum to introduce you and Elizabeth, but of course you weren't there." His voice grated.

Hannah made the mistake of meeting his gaze. The dark, almost fierce penetration of his eyes caused her to shiver.

"They know you rescued me and were eager to make your acquaintance."

Her heart turned over. "You've made too much of that experience. Anyone would have done what I did."

"No." His eyes had narrowed on her mouth. "Not anyone."

"I'm sorry I wasn't there." It would have been easier to say goodbye to him out there.

"I was, too," he said in a husky voice. "The meeting wasn't supposed to happen for another week, and we'd originally planned to meet in Rock Springs which would have been infinitely more convenient for me.

"Instead, I found myself missing you and your golden cherub, so I decided I didn't want to let any more time go by in case you both forgot me. But if you would prefer I left—"

"No—" she cried out. Her heart thudded in her chest. 'I mean—I appreciate your invitation, but I've already started dinner." She bit her lip before taking the plunge. "You're welcome to have it with me. It's just spaghetti."

His hands went to his hips in a purely male stance. Her suggestion seemed to have mollified him. "After eating in restaurants for months on end, that sounds like ambrosia."

Until he'd said so, Hannah hadn't stopped to consider that even for a man who could eat at five-star restaurants anytime he wished, there was no substitute for a home-cooked meal now and again.

"It'll be ready in a few minutes."

"Good. That gives me time to play with Elizabeth. I brought her a present. Where is she?"

"In her crib."

"Is she asleep?"

"I don't think so. I'll get her."

With her heart racing, Hannah hurried to the nursery. The baby was playing with her toes.

"I've got a big surprise for you, sweetheart. But don't get too excited because this is the last time we'll be seeing him." She gathered her in her arms and took her out to the living room.

As soon as the baby caught sight of Dominic's darkly handsome features, she recognized him at once and literally flung herself out of Hannah's arms to reach him. The gesture was done with such force, Hannah was taken completely off guard.

"*Elizabeth!*" she screamed in fright, but Dominic's swift reflexes prevented any accident from happening.

After chuckling he said, "I've missed you, too, *mignonne.*" He pressed tender kisses against her neck and cherubic face. "My friends were disappointed when they couldn't meet you. I've told them all about you."

At his words, a delicious shiver chased across Hannah's skin. She ached to feel his lips against her neck.

"As you've discovered, when you ask to see the baby, you do it at your own peril." The words came out in a teasing manner to cover the myriad feelings this man engendered. "I'm afraid Elizabeth has formed an attachment to you."

He flashed her an enigmatic smile that made her heart knock hard against her ribs. "I have no complaints. After such a loving greeting, I'm becoming addicted. In fact we like holding each other, don't we, *Petite*? Shall we ask your mommy to open your present? I want to see if it fits."

Guilt stabbed Hannah as she reached for the sack he'd left by a chair. He didn't know the baby was Lisa's.

When she'd thought she would never see him again, there'd been no reason to tell him.

Now that she knew there could never be a future with him, it wasn't necessary to divulge the truth.

Her hands shook as she pulled out a box gift-wrapped in a baby motif. Eagerly she undid the paper and lifted the lid. Inside the tissue was the most beautiful little yellow, two-piece cotton outfit she'd ever seen.

She held it up. Their eyes met over the embroidered neck. "It's perfectly adorable, Dominic."

A smile hovered around his lips. "*She's* adorable. Let's see how she looks in it."

"I think you'd better put it on her. If I try, we know what will happen."

He laughed deep in his throat. The sound thrilled her.

She placed the quilt on the couch so he could undress the baby. Elizabeth lay there contentedly blowing bubbles.

As Hannah handed him the new outfit she couldn't resist asking, "Where did you learn to handle babies so naturally?"

He got right to work. "My sister's first child turned out to be twin boys. For the first little while I'm afraid everyone had to pitch in."

She got the distinct impression he and his sister were close. Hannah would have loved to ask him more questions, but held back because he didn't offer anything more of a private nature.

"There," he murmured with a gleam of satisfaction in his eyes as he stood Elizabeth on her feet in her new outfit. "You're going to break a lot of hearts when you come of age, *ma belle*." He blew against her bare midriff where the top separated. It made the baby laugh out loud.

Hannah excused herself to check the sauce simmering on the stove. When she returned, she found him on the floor stretched out on his side with his head propped in one hand. Elizabeth lay next to him on her tummy, grabbing at ribbon from the package he held up for her. The scene tore at her heart.

It took everything Hannah possessed not to join them. Instead, she practiced self-control and sank down on the couch a few feet away. "Thank you for the generous gift, Dominic."

His eyes trapped hers. "I would do a great deal more if you would let me. It isn't every day someone throws all my good intentions back in my face."

She imagined he was talking about the five hundred dollars. "I'm sorry if that's the way it appeared to you."

"All's forgiven if you'll let me spend next weekend with you. I understand it's your Jubilee Days and there is a special parade in the town."

She held her breath for a moment. He might want a relationship with her, but she kept remembering that magazine article.

He's a sought after bachelor.

She held her breath for a moment. He might want a relationship with her, but she kept remembering that magazine article.

CHAPTER FOUR

"BY YOUR silence I assume you're going to be spending it with Elizabeth's father. How long have you two been lovers?" Dominic asked in a mild tone.

"What?"

"If I jumped to conclusions, I apologize." He went on teasing the baby.

Hannah puffed a pillow into place. "I haven't made any plans since I have to ride in the parade."

"I'd like to see that. So where is Elizabeth's father?"

The question caught her off guard. "I'm sure I don't know."

"But you're still in love with him."

"No!" she blurted, hot-faced, before she realized how revealing that sounded.

After a tension-filled silence, "If you really mean that, then should I assume you're reluctant to go out with me because you're afraid all men are cut from the same cloth as the baby's father? If that's true, then you're very much mistaken. When was the last time he visited her?''

They were on painful ground now. ''He's never seen Elizabeth.''

Dark lines shadowed his face. ''How long ago did he run off?'' The anger in Dominic's voice frightened her. It told volumes about his own character. No matter the circumstances, a child of Dominic Giraud's would never be abandoned or unloved.

Hannah leaned over and picked up the baby. ''He disappeared when he found out she was on the way.'' She kissed Elizabeth's temple. ''Having her wasn't part of his plan.''

Dominic muttered something in French beneath his breath, but it needed no translation because Hannah had muttered those same words in English too many times herself.

''Has he sent any money?''

She shook her head. ''He never had any, but we're managing, aren't we, sweetheart.''

''The bastard!''

''It's all right, Dominic. It's best that he's gone.''

His well-defined chest rose and fell. ''Does your sister live with you?''

A sharp pain entered her heart. ''Not for a while now.''

''But she helps out?''

"When she can," Hannah lied. "Dominic— If we're going to be able to enjoy our dinner in peace, I'd better put Elizabeth back to bed before she's gets too spoiled with your company."

"How did you know I was starving?" Dominic's deep, sensuous voice asked a few minutes later.

"You're a man, aren't you?"

His low laugh sent her hormone count out of range.

"If you'd like to sit there—" she indicated the table meant for two placed next to the wall. "You can start on your salad while I check on the bread warming in the oven."

The next twenty minutes were a revelation as she watched him put away three plates of spaghetti. Fortunately Elizabeth had fallen asleep quickly.

"I can't stop eating everything in sight. The meatballs are out of this world, and the bread…"

If his intention had been to make her feel good, he'd accomplished his objective. "Coming from a Frenchman, I'll take that as the supreme compliment."

"I wasn't patronizing you. Tell me what kind of bread this is," he asked after devouring another buttered slice. She couldn't believe he cared.

"It's an old Swedish recipe. It's not as good as authentic French bread, and I don't have any wine, but—"

"Don't do that again, Hannah!" he cut in on her abruptly.

"Do what?" Her fork paused midway to her mouth.

"Denigrate everything you do."

She blinked. "Is that what I've been doing?"

"You know you have," he ground out. "What that man did to you is criminal." Dominic sounded livid.

The fork dropped to her plate. She hated lying to Dominic, and the lies were compounding by the second. On a rush of guilty emotion she pushed herself away from the table and hurried over to the fridge for some store-bought ice cream.

Before she could pull the carton from the freezer compartment she felt a pair of strong, masculine hands slide on to her shoulders. He kneaded them with growing insistence. His touch made her lightheaded so she couldn't think clearly.

"Hannah—" he whispered in a husky voice, causing her legs to wobble. "Don't you realize I didn't say those things to upset you? Don't you know what kind of a woman you are?''

One of his hands had found its way to her neck. He caressed the skin below her ear. The wayward motion of his fingers gave her so much pleasure, he was driving her mad with it.

"I'm simply trying to understand how the man who fathered your child could have done what he did to you." She heard him pause for breath, as if he were having the greatest difficulty controlling his emotions. "Why are you holding back from me?"

"Dominic—" came her tortured cry, unable to go on like this any longer. But when she would have turned around to give in to the desire racking her body, they both heard the front doorbell chime at the same time.

He muttered a torrent of French words as she abruptly broke free of his hold. "Are you expecting someone?"

"No," she answered, so shaken by what had just transpired, her thought processes had grown sluggish. "I'd better see who it is before they ring again and waken the baby."

Her breathing shallow, she hurried through the apartment, aware of Dominic in quiet pursuit. Before she opened the door she stood on tiptoe to look through the peephole.

It was the P.I. assigned to Lisa's case. There had to have been a significant development, otherwise he would have phoned rather than come in person. What if it was bad news? Fear clutched at her heart. "Just a minute!"

She turned to Dominic. "I know who it is. Why don't you go back in the kitchen and help yourself to the ice cream? I won't be long."

The aggression in his stance illuminated another side of his nature. It came like a revelation that if he were ever crossed, he would make a formidable adversary.

"Are you sure you'll be all right?" His voice seemed to come from some dark, deep cavern.

"I'm positive."

She watched his teeth clench before he excused himself from the room with visible reluctance.

Her heart at her feet, she opened the door and went outside on the porch where their voices wouldn't be heard by Dominic or the baby.

"Bob? You obviously have something important to tell me."

The sandy-haired detective nodded. "I found your sister. She's in Fort Collins."

Hannah let out a gasp. "So close?" The college town was only an hour away in Colorado.

"Yes. From what the mechanic at a local garage told me, she came in with a college student named Steve Wright. They brought in a truck for repairs. The dent you described was there.

"The truck isn't the same color anymore, but it's yours. The mechanic gave me the phone number she gave them. I traced it to an address on Cache-Poudre Lane.

"I have no idea how long she's been at this address, or how long she'll stay. If you want to confront her, I suggest you drive there now." He handed her a folded piece of paper.

She clutched it in her palm. "I will. Thank you." Her eyes filled with liquid. "I can't thank you enough for all your help."

"You're welcome, Hannah. Good luck to you."

With tears of relief and trepidation running down her face, Hannah slipped back inside the apartment, colliding with Dominic who put his hands on her upper arms to steady her.

His eyes took in her wet pallor. "I heard a

man's voice. Was that Elizabeth's father? Did he threaten you in some way?''

"No!" she cried out. Because it was the truth, her voice rang with conviction.

His chest heaved. "Hannah, whatever this is, let me help you.''

She moistened her lips nervously. "Do you really mean it?'' Her voice shook.

"You can ask me that?'' he scathed.

Choosing her words carefully she said, "Dominic—there's something I have to do tonight. Someone I have to see.''

"You need me to stay with Elizabeth?''

Hannah shook her head. "No. She's going with me. I want you to go back to your friends.''

His body went rigid. "If you think I'm going to let you go anywhere alone with the baby at this time of night, then you don't know me at all. I'm not stepping foot outside this apartment unless it's with you. Now, we can go in my car or yours. The choice is up to you.''

Dominic's implacable will was too strong for Hannah right now. He meant what he said, and she was in too great a hurry to waste any time arguing when he would only win in the end.

"All right. Since the car seat is already in my car, let's take mine. You can drive."

The next few minutes were a blur as they packed up Elizabeth and hurried out to Hannah's parking space.

"Where are we going?" he asked as he pulled the car into traffic.

"Fort Collins. There's a turnoff as soon as we leave Laramie. It's not a freeway, but I think it's faster."

"Who's there you have to see in such a hurry?" he asked when they'd been driving for a while.

He had a right to know. She'd given him the right when she'd agreed to let him drive her. "My sister."

"I take it she's in some kind of trouble."

"I—I'm not sure."

He glanced over at her. "You look tired. Why don't you close your eyes and try to sleep. I'll wake you as soon as we get there."

Thankful that he wasn't pressing her for information, she did his bidding though she knew she would never sleep. Now that she was about to confront her sister, wretched memories she'd been repressing flooded her mind.

After Lisa had run away in Hannah's old truck, Hannah had talked Thornton's garage into putting a trailer hitch on the back of her car. Not a good idea for a compact, but she'd had no other choice if she wanted to pull her horse trailer and continue riding with the brigade.

The responsibility of caring for Elizabeth had put an end to nearly all of Hannah's extracurricular activities. But she'd drawn the line at giving up her horse, the one pleasure left to her.

"We're here, Hannah." *So soon?* Dominic squeezed her hand. The warmth of it radiated to her insides before he let go with seeming reluctance.

She opened her eyes. Sure enough a blue truck with the dent that had been there when she'd first purchased it stood in the driveway of a little bungalow.

"What can I do to help?"

"You've already done it by driving me. I won't be long."

She got out of the passenger seat and opened the back to reach for the baby. When she was well away from the car, Hannah kissed the little golden head bobbing next to her chin.

"This is it, sweetheart. You've grown so much, Lisa's not going to recognize you. In fact she's about to get the surprise of her life. Let's go.''

She walked up the porch steps with determination and rang the buzzer. Her watch said ten-thirty. Hannah didn't care how late it was. This moment had been months too long in coming.

The TV was on. Soon a nice-looking blond guy wearing shorts and sandals but no top, opened the door. He didn't look to be a day over twenty-one.

His blue eyes did a double take because he noticed right away the strong resemblance between her and Lisa despite the eight year difference in their ages.

''Hello. I'm Hannah Carr. If my sister Lisa is here, will you tell her I'd like to talk to her?''

He looked stunned. ''Sure. I'll get her. Just a minute.''

Hannah took several deep draughts of air while she waited. Five minutes must have passed before she heard footsteps.

''How did you find me?'' The angry question was the first thing Lisa said after she came out on the porch, shutting the door behind her. ''Come on. We can't talk here.''

Lisa hadn't changed. Hannah's heart sank

as she followed her sister's shorts- and shell-top-clad figure around the side of the house.

She swung around, her green eyes flashing with hostility. "What did you tell Steve?"

"Nothing. I simply asked him if my sister was here."

"Nothing else?"

"No."

"That's good, because Steve and I got married, and I don't want him to ever find out I had a baby."

With that revelation, any hope Hannah had entertained that when Lisa saw the child she'd given birth to over six months ago, her maternal instincts would take over, died an instant death.

"You're *married*?" She could hardly take it all in.

"Yes. The day I turned eighteen, and I don't want anything to wreck it."

"But Elizabeth's your baby, your flesh and blood!"

Lisa shook her head. "I wanted to get an abortion but you wouldn't let me. I told you in the hospital I wanted to put the baby up for adoption, but you said no. You thought I would change my mind, and you offered to take care of the baby until I realized I wanted her, remember?"

Hannah groaned, recalling everything...

"Well, that day never came for me, so I left. And now I have a real chance to be happy. Steve's the total opposite of dad. He doesn't tell me what to do. But if he ever found out I lied to him, he would leave me. Please don't tell him about *her*. Promise me, Hannah!"

That was all Elizabeth meant to Lisa. *Her*.

For the hundredth time she regretted that the two of them hadn't gone in for counseling after their father died, but there'd been so little money and Lisa would have refused.

"Look—I'm sorry I left without telling you where I was going, but I didn't know what else to do. I don't want her, Hannah. Go ahead and put her up for adoption."

The very idea of it made Hannah ill. "Lisa—"

"The baby deserves a family who really wants her. Just make sure she doesn't get the same kind of father we had."

For Hannah, this conversation was worse than any nightmare. "What will you tell your husband about the baby? He's seen me with Elizabeth and probably assumes she's your niece."

"I'll just say that because there's no husband, you wanted to tell me you've decided to place her for adoption. There's no problem with that.''

Hannah lowered her head to kiss Elizabeth's forehead. "Did you even tell Steve you had a sister?"

"Of course. I'll just pretend that you never wanted him to learn you had a baby. He knows about our lives, about Dad. He knows you're in school, that we look a lot alike. I told him you're an expert rider. You can believe me or not, but one day soon I was planning to get in touch with you.

"Before I left home, I knew you'd fight me on the subject of adoption. That's why I wanted to wait awhile, until you got sick and tired of tending her. There's no way you can go on watching out for a baby and finish up your schooling. Your visit has saved me a phone call. How did you find me, anyway?"

Oh, Lisa... "The truck. I had it traced."

"Oops. Sorry about that. I'll give it back as soon as Steve buys us a car."

"It's all right. Consider it a belated wedding present from me," she whispered brokenly.

"I guess you figured I stole your ID, too. I'm sorry, but I needed it to get a job here in Fort Collins. I knew you could get a duplicate really fast."

So that was where her license had gone.

"You've been here the whole time?"

"Yes. I make pizzas. That's how Steve and I met. He's a driver for the same company, trying to put himself through college. I'm going to help him, and then he's going to help me. We rarely get time off together. You're lucky to have found us home.

"Listen, Hannah. If you give the baby to a nice family who's dying for a child, then maybe you'll meet a professor or something at the university. You're almost twenty-seven with no marriage prospects in sight.

"Every woman should have the chance to find the man of her dreams. One day you'll meet yours, but not if you're stuck in the apartment making baby formula and changing diapers."

Hannah weaved in place.

I've met mine. But there won't be a future for us.

Hannah did know one thing, however. When fate sent Dominic away, no other man would ever matter to her again. If Lisa were ever to meet him, she would understand why he'd spoiled Hannah for anyone else.

"Steve's waiting. I've got to go in. Have you got my phone number?" Hannah nodded once more. "Good. As soon as you contact an adoption agency and they tell us what to do, call me so I can sign the papers.

"Steve works two jobs, but I don't leave for work until three. The best time to get me is around noonish. I'll tell Steve we decided to meet for lunch or something."

While Hannah stood there in shock, Lisa kissed her cheek. "It's really good to see you again. Take care. Love ya." Never even acknowledging the baby, she ran back to the house.

Tears poured down Hannah's face. She clutched Elizabeth to her heart. "How could I possibly give you up now, sweetheart? I can't bear it."

When she reached the car, Dominic was waiting for her. By tacit agreement he relieved her of the baby and put her in the car seat.

Once he'd taken his place behind the wheel it was too late for Hannah to dash the moisture from her lashes. His all-encompassing glance had already registered the anguished state of her emotions.

"Obviously something traumatic has happened to you."

"Dominic—" she began in a shaky voice. "I realize you mean well, but t—this is something private. I can't talk about it right now. Please take us home.''

With an almost imperceptible nod of his dark head, he started the car and they retraced the route back to Laramie in silence. In no condition to handle the kind of inquisition he had in mind once they arrived, she reached for the baby and started up the stairs.

"Hannah?" She heard footsteps behind her.

She hurriedly undid the lock and practically ran through the apartment to put Elizabeth to bed. Dominic was waiting for her in the hall when she came out of the bedroom a few minutes later.

In the dim light they faced each other like adversaries. Too much pain had broken her down. She started to shake and couldn't seem to stop.

His hands shot out to grasp her shoulders. She tried to back away from him, but he held her fast. "Tell me what's wrong, Hannah. Every time I touch you, you tremble. Whatever your ex-lover did to you, don't you know I would never hurt you?"

Hannah realized they'd reached the point where she could no longer allow him to think things that were patently untrue.

"I don't have an ex-lover!" she cried out.

"I've never had *any* lover!" Using all her strength, she managed to break free of his hold.

His powerful body stilled instantly. "What are you saying?"

"Elizabeth's not my baby! She's my *sister's!*"

"Mon Dieu!"

Struggling for breath, she explained, "Lisa was only seventeen when she got involved with a man who left Laramie the second he heard she was expecting.

"She never wanted the baby, but I prevented her from getting an abortion. As soon as Elizabeth was born, she wanted to put her up for adoption. Again I said no, so Lisa ran away. I paid a private investigator to find her. Tonight he traced her to an address in Fort Collins. I drove there to talk to her and let her see how beautiful Elizabeth is."

Fresh tears trickled down her cheeks. "But Lisa doesn't want her. She didn't even look at Elizabeth or try to hold her! Two months ago my sister got married to a college student named Steve Wright who has no idea she ever had a baby. I've been told to put her up for adoption!"

As great heaving sobs shook her body, she felt Dominic's strong arms go around her.

Too emotionally drained to fight him, she soon discovered it was heaven to melt into this man's hard-muscled strength.

His compact physique seemed to absorb her pain. But it was more than that. Much more. In his arms she felt safe and protected from the cares of the world. She'd never known this kind of security before in her life.

But while Dominic's hands roved over her back, and he whispered soothing words in French in his intention to comfort her, other sensations began making themselves known to Hannah.

Though she'd had several semi-serious relationships with men in her early twenties, never once had she felt this raw kind of desire that swept away every inhibition.

Being in Dominic's arms made her lose cognizance of everything going on around her. Shaken by primitive needs only he had aroused and could satisfy, she discovered her body trying to get closer to him. Her mouth longed to know the taste of his.

"Hannah—" he cried.

She didn't know why he'd called out her name like that, but it woke her up to the fact that she was out of control.

"Forgive me," she whispered, trying to ease away from him. "Aren't you sorry you hung around tonight to see me break down like this?'' She laughed grimly.

"Sorry—" His eyes blazed dark fire. "*Mon Dieu!* what are you talking about?'' His hands had slid to her upper arms. He shook her with refined savagery. "I wanted to stay in your arms from the moment you rescued me.'' His voice sounded ragged with desire. "But tonight you're in pain, and though there's nothing I desire more than to kiss us both into oblivion, this isn't the time or the place.

"When we do come together, I'm going to make certain there's nothing to disturb us for weeks on end. Do you understand what I'm saying?'' The cords stood out in his neck.

"Yes,'' she whispered as her heart plummeted. He was talking about an affair...

It would be so easy.

Until it was over.

Dear God. The pain would be unending.

He took a fortifying breath. "I asked you to spend next weekend with me, but I don't want to wait that long to see you again. We have to talk.'' His hands were kneading her flesh, creating little whirlpools of desire that radiated through her body.

"As soon as I get back to the hotel, I'll work things out with the guys. We have to go out of town again, but I can be back Monday night. I'll come by the apartment around six. Until then, don't let anything happen to you."

He caught her face between his hands. She knew what was coming. If she didn't stop him now, it would be too late.

"No! Please don't!" she cried, pushing hard against his chest to prevent his mouth from capturing hers.

His expression was incredulous. "What's wrong, Hannah?"

"Everything," she whispered, rubbing her arms nervously as she backed away from him. Though it was killing her, she knew she had to break it off with him now.

"You're a remarkable man, and I've enjoyed getting to know you so much. But my life is very complicated, and tonight has to be the last time we see each other.

"Don't ask me why. It's nothing to do with you personally. The reasons are only important to me."

Afraid she would give in to the cravings that racked her body, she hurried to the door and opened it.

"What if I don't want to go?" The question came out more like a hiss.

"Even if you're not welcome?" She flung

the brutal question at him. It hung like a live wire between them, but he'd left her with no other choice.

His body tautened. "You really want this to be goodbye?"

"Yes," she affirmed boldly, though she was dying inside. "I've tried discouraging you from the beginning. At this point I don't know how to make it any clearer.

"You've more than paid me back for the night of the accident by taking me to dinner and buying that little outfit for Elizabeth. But now it's over."

Beneath his tan she could tell his handsome face had lost some of its color. "Hannah—" He said her name in what sounded like a tortured whisper.

By the greatest strength of will she stayed frozen in place, praying he wouldn't see through her desperate facade. "Please go."

He rubbed the back of his neck. "Will you at least answer me one more question?"

She swallowed hard. "What is it?"

"How soon are you going to place her for adoption?"

"I'm getting the process started on Monday. My attorney, Mr. Moench, will know what to do. If I hadn't been so headstrong, Lisa wouldn't have run away and

Elizabeth would be with parents who love her right now.

"I've made every mistake in the book. As it is, I've kept her too long and have probably done irreparable damage. No doubt she'll have difficulty bonding with anyone else."

"And what about you?" Dominic demanded in a thick tone. "How are *you* going to handle giving her up?"

She closed her eyes tightly against the compassion in his voice. *That's the question that is killing me, and you better than any other person alive knows it.*

"Fortunately it's not your worry. You have a bullet train to build. *Au revoir*, Dominic," she said in her best French and quietly shut the door on him.

It's over.

Everything's over.

CHAPTER FIVE

THE LAWYER sat back in his swivel chair, his fingertips beneath his chin. "Hannah? I know you love that baby as if she were your own. Before you take any steps to have her placed with a family, have you considered asking your sister how she would feel if *you* adopted her?"

She hugged the baby a little tighter. "I couldn't sleep all night thinking about it. But I'm through trying to tell Lisa what to do. I never had the right, and I can't imagine her saying yes when she has fought so hard to put her old life behind her. Elizabeth would be a constant reminder of the pain my sister wants to forget," she said mournfully.

"Nevertheless, may I suggest you contact her and simply ask the question before you bring her to my office to sign papers?"

"I'm afraid of hurting her any more."

"Hannah— It's my obligation to make certain every avenue is explored before a legal decision is made. We're talking here about a child's whole future, and what is best for her. Give your sister a chance to express her feelings on the subject. Then at least you won't have to add more guilt to your pain."

"What do you mean?"

"I fear that if you don't broach the subject with Lisa, you will always be haunted by what-if? At least if she says no, you'll have your definitive answer and learn to live with it."

Mr. Moench's insistence about this surprised her. It was as if he could see into her psyche and know what was going on without her having to say a word.

Puzzled by his insight, she got up to leave. "I'll think about it and get back to you. Thank you for fitting me in without a prior appointment."

"It's my pleasure."

After thanking him, she left his office to get back to the apartment. The baby needed to go down for her nap. Hannah had thought about opening the museum for the afternoon, but couldn't bring herself to do it. The dreadful emptiness inside her seemed to have grown to an acute stage. She could barely function.

No doubt Dominic was far away from Laramie by now. If he ever did return, it would be for business and she would never know about it. The thought of never seeing him again was tearing her apart.

As for Elizabeth...

Though Hannah fought the attorney's advice, she knew he was right. For the sake of closure, she had to ask her sister the question.

Before she lost courage, she reached in her purse for Lisa's phone number, then hurried to the kitchen to make the call. A few minutes into the conversation and she almost fainted when her sister said, "Hannah? You idiot! Of course you're the one I would want to adopt her, but I wasn't going to suggest it unless you asked!"

Hannah couldn't believe what she was hearing.

"You've always been more self-sacrificing than most people. I knew you loved her, but I didn't want you to go on taking care of my problem if it wasn't what you really wanted. I'm glad you want her. Now I'll be able to love her from a distance, just like an aunt, and I won't have to wonder how she's doing, or what's happening to her."

"You mean that? You're not just saying it?"

"Hannah—haven't you been listening to me?"

"Yes." her voice caught. "But you've just given me a priceless gift."

"Hannah, I'm so sorry for the way I acted the other night. I was just so shocked to see you. When I saw Elizabeth, I have to admit I was glad you made me go through with my pregnancy. She's beautiful. Steve thinks she looks exactly like both of us."

"She does." Hannah half laughed, half sobbed in relief and thanksgiving.

"But how will you raise her? It'll ruin your plans for school, and the earnings from that pitiful museum won't help you out during the winter months when it's closed."

"I don't care about that," Hannah cried with happiness. "I'll work things out."

"Why don't you sell the property?"

"What?"

"It's never meant a thing to me sitting there. I bet we could get a lot of money for it. Dad made us live like misers, but now that he's gone, there's nothing to stop us. At this point Steve and I would give anything for some financial help. You remember Judy Finnegan. Her dad Ray sells real estate out of their home. If you want, I'll call him right now and find out what he thinks it's worth."

Hannah paused for a moment, remembering her promise to her father. But when she thought of the joy of having Elizabeth as her own little girl, she told her sister to go ahead and contact Ray Finnegan, then call her back.

In the interim, Hannah phoned Mr. Moench's law firm and left a message with his secretary to thank him for his good advice. The next time she came in to his office, it would be to adopt Elizabeth herself.

"Hannah?" her sister said an hour later, sounding upset. "Bad news. Ray's not optimistic about finding a buyer who would want the museum, as well. Being that it's on the state historical register, it could take several years, maybe longer for someone to come along who would appreciate it and pay us what it's worth.

"But he said he'd be happy to list it and see what happens. A buyer could call in tomorrow and prove him wrong. You'll have to go over to their house and sign some papers."

"I'll do that," Hannah assured her sister before they hung up. But while she was doing the wash later, she realized two years was too long to wait for money they all needed right now.

Inevitably her thoughts turned to Dominic, who'd wanted the legal right to use their land. Did he want it badly enough to buy their property?

Realizing where her thoughts were headed, she chastised herself for entertaining them after what she'd been through saying goodbye to him. To start everything up again would be like dying a second death.

But since Lisa's phone call, it came to her that maybe Mr. Finnegan could approach Dominic so Hannah didn't have to deal with him. The Realtor could represent her family in a purely business transaction.

She wasn't so naive that she didn't realize he was hoping she would give him permission to run the train across her property. He'd admitted that he often had to wait for a hesitant landowner to finally cave in.

Most likely Dominic wouldn't be interested. But it was worth a try as long as she didn't have to see or talk to him in person.

"Zane— It's Dominic. Something came up," he muttered, putting on his sunglasses. Driving due west into a sun that would be setting in another hour was playing havoc with his mother-of-all-headaches. "I won't be in Tooele until late, so don't plan on dinner. How about breakfast in the morning instead?"

He clicked off before pulling his Jeep on to the freeway from the exit leading out of

Evanston for the Utah border. The rest of the calls which had piled up on his answering service over the weekend could be returned tomorrow. Right now he was doing well to be going in the right direction.

A minute later his cell phone rang. Relieved for such a quick response, he reached for it and automatically said Zane's name.

"Hello? Mr. Giraud?"

It wasn't Zane. "That's right."

"This is Ray Finnegan. I'm a Realtor in Laramie, Wyoming. I'm representing two sisters, a Ms. Carr and Mrs. Wright, who have put their property on the market."

Hannah? He almost drove off the road.

"They tell me you showed an interest in the property to lay track for a bullet train. I've been hearing about that project from other people. It's an exciting idea. Anyway, these ladies thought they would give you first option to buy before it's officially listed with me."

Mon Dieu. He knew she would never sell that land unless something dire had forced her to let go of it.

No matter that she'd practically thrown him out of her apartment to make certain he never came back, Dominic knew in his gut she had to care about him on some level, or at least care about his project, otherwise this Realtor wouldn't have contacted him at all.

He gripped the cell phone tighter. "I *am* interested, but I'm out of town at the moment. Don't do anything until I get in touch with you."

"That's fine. I'll wait to hear from you then."

After they clicked off, Dominic made an illegal U-turn through the vegetation dividing the freeway in order to get back to Evanston in the shortest time possible. En route he placed another call to Zane, advising him he wouldn't be coming to Tooele at all. He would explain everything later.

With that call made, he asked the operator to connect him with the airport. In case there wasn't an early evening flight to Laramie from Evanston, he would charter one, and make sure there was a rental car available to him on the other end. He didn't have the patience to wait for the time it would take him to drive back there again.

Hannah's brutal rejection of him had knocked him sideways. After leaving a confidential message on Mr. Moench's answering machine, he'd checked out of his hotel and had driven across the state in an effort to blot all thoughts of her from his consciousness.

When that hadn't succeeded, he'd stayed in his motel room for the last two nights, and had proceeded to get well and truly drunk, something he hadn't done since the ugly, definitive confrontation with his amoral father ten years ago.

That hadn't worked, either. He'd awakened a few hours ago in more emotional pain than he'd thought possible.

Before this unexpected call, he'd planned to wait a few days, then phone Hannah's attorney to find out what was happening with Elizabeth before he showed up at the museum again.

Now that timetable had changed!

He and Ms. Carr were destined to have a long talk, but not over the phone, and not with her sister or a third party involved. It was going to be face-to-face, even if he had to break down the door to get to her and the baby.

Dominic could always count on a loving welcome from Elizabeth. The look of worship in those precious green eyes, her cupid smile, were all that had kept him going since her elusive, green-eyed angel *aunt* had shut the door in his face.

*   *   *

"Is it serious, doctor?"

"No. Your little girl has caught a cold, but if you'll put a steamer in her room and give her this infant cold medicine, she'll be fine in a few days."

Relieved that Elizabeth's condition wasn't serious, Hannah thanked the doctor and headed for the drugstore.

This was the first time she'd been forced to take the baby to the nighttime pediatric clinic for an emergency. But she'd sounded so croupy all of a sudden out at the museum, Hannah hadn't dared wait until morning to get her in to see the pediatrician.

"Hannah?" she heard a familiar male voice call to her as she drove into her parking space at the apartment.

She jerked around in disbelief. It was Dominic! The joy of seeing him made chaos of the pitiful defenses she'd tried in vain to erect against her feelings for him.

His presence meant he'd received the call from Ray Finnegan. Somewhere deep inside she'd had a feeling he would come in person to talk to her about sale of the property. She just hadn't expected it to be tonight!

"H-how long have you been waiting here?" Her voice faltered.

"Long enough to wonder if I should drive

out to the museum in case you were in some kind of trouble. Elizabeth sounds ill.''

Hannah reached in back for her. ''She has a cold. I've just come from the doctor.''

''How can I help?''

Her breath caught in her throat. ''If you wouldn't mind bringing her diaper bag and that sack with the steamer, I'd appreciate it.''

''Of course.''

He followed her up the steps. This time she jammed the key in the front door lock to be sure it would open so there'd be no chance of his touching her hand to assist her. After the other night, she feared the slightest contact would set her body on fire.

''Shall I fill the steamer from the bathroom or the kitchen?'' he inquired smoothly, as if they'd spent the whole weekend together. *As if there'd been no goodbye scene at all.*

''The kitchen,'' she called after him from the baby's bedroom, not wanting him to see she'd left her hose to dry on the towel rack in the bathroom.

While she got Elizabeth ready for bed, he entered the room and placed the steamer on her dresser. After plugging it in, he handed Hannah the medicine, then leaned over to kiss the baby.

"Sleep well, *mignonne*," she heard him murmur before he left the room.

Elizabeth recognized him and cried harder for a minute. But Hannah distracted her long enough to make her take her medicine, then gave her a bottle of juice. At first the baby fought the nipple, but with persistence Hannah was finally able to prop the bottle and get her to start drinking.

Slowly she tiptoed to the door and shut off the light. Blessed quiet reigned. But to her chagrin another kind of storm had been building inside Hannah's body since Dominic had shown up at her apartment.

She ached to touch him, to be held by him again. How much longer could she pretend indifference before he sensed her desire?

Taking a deep breath to keep her unassuaged longings at bay, she finally found the courage to walk in the living room, hoping to convey a nonchalance she didn't feel.

His hard, masculine frame lounged back in her father's favorite chair, looking insolently at ease. Dark penetrating eyes swept over her face and figure clad in jeans and a plaid blouse. Her heart beat such a swift tattoo, she wondered if he could hear it.

"Would you like a soft drink or coffee?"

"Maybe later," he murmured. "Right now

I want to know why you need cash so badly, you're willing to sell your birthright. Assuming you went to your attorney to put the baby up for adoption, is it possible your sister decided you could keep Elizabeth in exchange for an exorbitant amount of money? Is that what this decision to part with your land is all about?''

''No!'' she cried out, hugging her arms to her waist. ''Nothing like that, Dominic, though I can understand how you might have come to that conclusion.

''It's true I went to see Mr. Moench. He told me to talk to Lisa about adopting the baby myself before things went any further. I have to admit I was surprised he understood the situation so well. Without his suggestion, I wouldn't have found the courage to phone my sister. Thank heaven I did!'' she said emotionally.

''To my joy, Lisa wants me to keep Elizabeth!''

Dominic's eyes gleamed in the soft light of the living room. ''That's the best news I've heard in a long time.''

Hannah nodded, never doubting his sincerity. ''But she realizes I don't have the kind of money it takes to really care for a baby and raise it, so she suggested we sell the property and divide the proceeds.

"My sister is much more practical and modern than I am. As she pointed out, they need financial help to get through school, and I need funds to be a full-time mother to the baby. The museum is not the answer, which is something I've always known.

"The more I thought about it, the more her arguments made sense. So I called Ray Finnegan. Unfortunately he thinks it could be a couple of years before a buyer comes along who will want the land and museum, too."

Unexpectedly she saw Dominic rise to his feet. "And you need the money now, so you thought to contact me." He finished the sentence for her.

She was afraid to look at him.

"Yes, because you once told me that you sometimes buy property for your bullet train project when there's no other alternative."

"I did say that," he murmured, moving closer. "Why didn't you contact me yourself?"

Without realizing it, she had started to back away from him, but her legs bumped into the edge of an end table. "Because I wanted this to be a purely business proposition. Naturally

I understand that you don't want the property for yourself, but only as a means to an end.

"That's why I instructed Mr. Finnegan to set up a contract where he would be agents for both of us. He would charge you a fair and equitable market price. On my part, I would pay you interest until he found the right buyer to take the property off your hands and still allow you to lay track.

"I—I hoped—" She could scarcely keep her train of thought when he stood this close to her. "I assumed both of us might benefit from the transaction through the Realtor without your having to come back to Laramie and be bothered.

"As you pointed out to me, you still have hundreds, maybe thousands of people to contact the further west you go. The last thing I wanted to do was take you away from your work."

His hands lifted to her face. He cupped her cheeks, forcing her head up until she had no choice but to meet his searching gaze.

"So you didn't say goodbye to me because you never wanted to see me again, but only because you didn't want to disturb me from something you thought was more important to me."

"Yes— No— You're twisting my words,

Dominic.'' She tried not to look at him, afraid of what he could read in her eyes. ''I meant it to be goodbye.''

''Because you have no personal interest in me.''

''That's right.'' She grabbed at the safety net he'd thrown her.

''Then before I go, you won't mind a simple kiss to seal our business arrangement. Naturally with a man I draw the line at a handshake, but since you're a woman, I'll make the exception.''

''Please don't, Domi—'' But the rest of her panicked entreaty was smothered as his mouth covered hers with primitive force, cutting off any hope of escape.

Hannah moaned from the depth of such intense passion. This was no gentle, experimental foray of the senses, no testing of the waters. There was a mutual explosion of need that melded her body to his, allowing him to drink deeply with no thought of denial.

He hadn't told her he loved her. He'd promised her nothing. But he *did* want her. She knew that without him having to say the words. Though it would only hurt her in the end, she'd wanted to taste and feel him like this for so long. To finally be able to hold him like this...

Caught up in a swirl of mindless ecstasy, her hands slid up his chest to wrap around his neck. She couldn't get enough of him any other way, not when he was so much taller than she.

On a groan, he gathered her body in his arms. She sensed where he was taking her, but she was too on fire for him, too caught up in sensual need to obey the tiny voice of warning deep inside that was her conscience.

After tonight she would never see him again. But for the hours of darkness left to them, her only desire was to pour out the love she had to give on this remarkable man, the one great love of her life.

"Hannah—" He cried her name over and over again as he carried her into the bedroom. "There's so much I have to say to you, *mon amour*. But after waiting this long to get you in my arms like this, I'm burning alive."

"So am I," she admitted feverishly, worshiping his face and neck with her lips. "Every time you kiss Elizabeth, I imagine you kissing me. It's been a torture I could hardly bear."

In the soft light from the lamp she'd left on earlier, his dark eyes blazed with desire. "Then you have some idea how it has been for me watching her cling to you. Do you have any comprehension of how many times I wished myself in her place?''

He followed her down on the bed, devouring her mouth, sending a voluptuous warmth through her trembling body. His hands slid into her hair. She felt his fingers tighten around her curls.

''Mon Dieu!'' he cried in a low, husky voice, ''I've wanted you since the night I saw your beautiful face and felt your arms go around me. At the time I may have only been semiconscious, but the imprint of your gorgeous body against mine set up a craving nothing else will ever satisfy.''

His lips roved her face, her eyes, her nose, cheeks and hair. ''I want you with every breath that's in me. I could eat you alive, that's how hungry I am for you. You want me the same way, so don't bother to deny it.'' His mouth closed over hers with shocking ferocity.

''I don't deny anything.'' Her voice throbbed when he allowed her space to breathe. ''If you stopped kissing me now, I think I'd die. I'm in love with you, Dominic.'' The confession was out before she could stop it.

They were both so caught up in the throes of passion, she thought he might not have heard her. But in time his hands stilled their caressing movements, leaving her writhing for more.

He lifted his head to look into her eyes. "Say that again?" His breathing was as ragged as hers.

"My honesty has changed everything, hasn't it?" She tried to get off the bed, but he tightened his hold so she couldn't move.

"On the contrary. I want to hear it all."

No you don't, an inner voice cried. Unfortunately, it was too late to backtrack. "I'm in love with you," came her quiet admission. "I loved you from the first moment I saw you lying in the grass. But I never wanted you to find out because I knew you could never love someone like me."

His expression darkened. "What do you mean, someone like you?"

She couldn't understand why he sounded so angry.

"Please don't pretend to misunderstand, Dominic," she begged as tears smarted her eyes. She fought to keep them from falling. "I'm not as naive as my sister who was so desperate for love, she talked herself into believing that Elizabeth's father would marry her.

"Right now you feel a temporary attraction

to me, but I'm under no illusion that a man with your dreams and responsibilities is suddenly going to fall in love, let alone shed his bachelorhood for me and a baby who isn't even his.''

Something flickered in the recesses of his beautiful brown eyes.

''You're wrong, you know,'' he muttered emotionally.

Before she could countenance it, he'd produced a ring from his pocket. A gasp escaped her lips as he slid it on the ring finger of her left hand. The exquisite pear-shaped stone in a light emerald color shimmered in the soft light, dazzling her eyes.

She stared up into his. *''Domin—''* she started to say, but he kissed her trembling mouth quiet. ''The night of my accident, I fell in love with a green-eyed angel. By the next day I had fallen in love with her tiny, green-eyed cherub. After I left Laramie the first time, I knew I had to have you both, or nothing in my life would ever make sense again.''

Hannah shook her head. ''This just can't be happening to me.'' She clung to him, unable to credit that he was in love with her, that he'd already bought a ring.

''Believe it,'' came his intense whisper. After another kiss that blotted out the world, he traced the singing curve of her mouth with his finger. "If I wasn't in love, why do you think I kept coming back no matter how many times you tried to get rid of me?"

She caught his hand to her mouth to kiss it. "You know the only reason I pushed you away was because I was afraid you would find out how much I loved you. I couldn't have borne your pity."

He sucked in his breath. "Pity was the last thing on my mind, *chérie*. Now that I know you feel exactly the same way I do, how soon do you think Elizabeth will be well enough to travel?"

Hannah was so on fire for him, she was practically incoherent. "In a few days," she answered in a daze. "Why?"

"That will give us enough time to see about her adoption before we leave the country."

She tried to sit up. "Where are we going?"

"To the place where I was born in the South of France."

He was taking her to his home.

"But I don't have a passport or—"

"Sh-h-h." He gave her another soul-searching kiss. "I'll arrange a special visa and license so we can be married in Vence where my mother will be able to witness our nuptials. I can't wait for you to get acquainted with each other.

"Elizabeth's going to be her first granddaughter. *Maman* will adore both of you on sight. As for my sister Nicole and her family, they'll be overjoyed. In fact both of them will fight to tend the baby while we slip away for a honeymoon. My three-year-old nephews will find their little blond American cousin pure delight."

"I long to meet all your relatives," Hannah's voice trembled, but she was too transformed by his love to ask about the father he hadn't mentioned yet. The word honeymoon had filled her mind with pictures, sending a thrill through her body. Over and over she lifted her mouth to meet the unbridled hunger of his.

He buried his face in her golden curls. "Everyone is going to adore you, *mon amour*. As for your family, I'm every bit as anxious to meet your sister and her husband. If you want to include them in our wedding plans, nothing would please me more. But because Elizabeth is such a sensitive issue," he murmured, raising his head to look down at her, "I'm leaving that decision up to you."

Her luminescent green eyes searched his. "I adore you for saying that. To be honest, I think it would be better for Lisa if we announced our news after the fact.''

"I believe that's the wisest decision, too, *chérie*. When we return to Laramie, you can introduce us. If your sister is amenable, maybe we could host a reception for all of your friends to celebrate both marriages. Since we'll be living in Laramie, I want to meet everyone important to you.''

Hannah had been listening to his plans for them with a sense of wonder. His generosity of spirit, the part of him that wanted to include her sister and make her happy, too, caused Hannah to love him all the more.

But the mention of Laramie brought her back to earth in a hurry. After what she'd learned about him in that magazine, the idea of him settling down in Wyoming because of *her* was ludicrous!

"I couldn't ask that of you, Dominic. Laramie is a vastly different proposition from New York or France.''

He grazed her earlobe with his teeth. "I couldn't agree with you more. Laramie is where I found you, which makes it my favorite place on the planet.''

"Bu—"

"No buts.'' He stopped the rest of her words with his mouth. "I never expected to fall in love, let alone get married. Now that I've found the woman I didn't believe existed, I intend to make you as happy as you make me."

"I'd be happy with you anywhere!" she declared from the bottom of her heart. "But think, Dominic— It would be too great a sacrifice for you to have to live in Laramie on a permanent basis. There's nothing here! In time you would learn to hate it, and eventually hate me." Her voice shook.

"You're wrong, Hannah." The tone in his voice warned her to leave it alone. "I fell in love with a Wyoming woman. As soon as I make you my wife, I plan to become an integral part of your life. Your family is here, your pioneer roots. How would you like it if we built a home on your property?"

She gasped softly before easing herself out of his arms so she could get to her feet. It was impossible to think with him constantly kissing her. Right now they needed to sort out something vital, and that meant putting a little distance between them.

"You already know the answer to that question. I feel like I'm in a fantastic dream where all the desires of my heart are about to come true. But marriage means you have to compromise, so both parties are content. You have family in France, so don't pretend that your roots don't run as deeply as mine.''

A shadow passed over his handsome features. He levered his powerful body from the bed and came to stand in front of her. As his hands started to reach for her, she backed away from him.

''I can't concentrate when you touch me, Dominic.''

''That's good,'' he muttered with a devilish smile before pulling her into his arms. ''I don't want you to think, *mon amour.* Just listen.'' His lips caressed the side of her neck.

''Of course I feel a strong bond to my heritage. But my past is associated with a great deal of pain, which is why I moved to New York.''

What pain?

Since he appeared to have a loving relationship with his mother and sister, then it had to be another woman who had hurt him so badly he couldn't remain in the same country with her.

Someone wealthy and cultured. Beautiful. All the things a man of his stature and influence would want in a mate.

Was that why he'd chosen Hannah? Because she was the *exact opposite* of everything he'd once desired? An average-looking girl who knew her place in the scheme of things and would feel out of her element in any other ambience?

Had his gratitude over her playing the good Samaritan, coupled with his strong instinct to protect Elizabeth, been the deciding factors in this incredible marriage proposal?

"As wonderful as New York is," he said, unaware of her turmoil, "it has never been home to me. Until the night of my accident when you held me in your arms, no woman has ever has made me want to put down new roots. Meeting you has transformed my life, *mon amour.*"

"It's the same for me," she whispered. "I—I love you so much, Dominic. I just hope you won't live to regret this decision."

Tension emanated from his rock-hard physique. "How could I possibly do that when you and Elizabeth are my very life?" His voice throbbed with emotion.

"Speaking of our daughter-to-be, I heard her cough. Let's go in and tell her we're about to become a family." With his hands on her shoulders from behind, he urged Hannah forward to the baby's room.

Elizabeth was awake, but she didn't sound quite as congested as when Hannah had put her down earlier, thank heaven. As soon as the baby saw Dominic, her arms started to flail. Within seconds her precious face screwed up for a good cry, to make sure she had his full attention.

Hannah recognized that look and broke into laughter. Dominic's deep-throated chuckle reverberated throughout the nursery, as well.

"Come here to me, Elizabeth." He picked her up and held her in front of his chest with one hand beneath her head, the other supporting her firm little body. Immediately she stopped crying.

"Your mommy has made me the happiest man alive by agreeing to become my wife. That means you're going to be *ma petite fille*. How does that sound to you?"

The look of adoration in the baby's eyes and smile led Hannah to believe Elizabeth understood, and was giving him her wholehearted approval.

Dominic's gaze suddenly locked with Hannah's. The glow coming from those black-brown depths couldn't be mistaken for any other emotion than love.

To have Dominic Giraud for her father made Elizabeth the luckiest little girl on earth.

Would that he loved Hannah as completely.

But she refused to lie to herself about the truth of his feelings for her. How long her love would be able to hold him was a question she couldn't answer.

It depended on many factors, not the least of which was the fact that despite his protestations, once the honeymoon was over, Laramie would begin to lose its charm.

She shuddered to think what life would be like when *she* no longer charmed him, either...

"What's wrong, Hannah?"

His question jerked her out of her tortured thoughts. She clung to the crib railing. "Nothing."

He'd been speaking French to the baby, so it surprised Hannah to discover that he'd come to stand next to her, his thigh brushing against hers provocatively. "Don't pretend everything's fine when I know differently. What's on your mind?" he whispered against her neck, sending a river of delight coursing through her veins.

"I just think you ought to reconsider your decision about settling in Laramie," she said, unable to look at him. "Maybe New York isn't your favorite place, but it's where you work. Elizabeth and I would be perfectly happy living there with you.

"I may not have visited it yet, but I do know it's one of the most exciting cities in the world in which to live. There's so much to see and do, you could never be bored, and—"

"We'll vacation there from time to time," he broke in before she could finish, "but I already consider this place home."

No you don't, darling. France is your true home. You're just saying these things to please me, she cried inwardly.

Before she broke down in front of him, she excused herself to fill the steamer with more water.

He was trying.

He was doing everything in his power to make her happy.

But she knew who he really was. That knowledge changed everything because one day soon he would realize what he'd given up to marry her.

When that happened, he would want to move on. *Alone.* Her world would be shattered for all time.

The alternative was to give him back the ring tonight and sever the relationship for good.

But how could she do that when she was so in love with him, she couldn't imagine life without him now...

CHAPTER SIX

Dear Lisa,

I'm sending you this letter by Express Air from St. Paul de Vence, France, so you won't wonder where I am. By the time you receive it, I'll be married to the man of my dreams, and Elizabeth will have a father.

HANNAH refrained from saying anything about the adoption. That could come later when she and Lisa met privately in the lawyer's office.

The only reason I haven't spoken of Dominic Giraud before now is because I hoped, but never believed he would propose to me. Once he did, everything happened so fast, I still feel like I'm in a dream.

We met one evening when he had a Jeep accident by the river behind the museum. I fell madly in love with him. He and his friends have plans to build a bullet train across the U.S. He wanted permission to run track over our land. One thing led to another. It was love at first sight for him and Elizabeth. I think he's marrying me so he can have her for his own daughter.

Tomorrow the private ceremony will take place in a little church filled with fifteenth-century frescoes Dominic discovered as a boy while he was out hiking. It's called Chapelle Sainte Elizabeth, if you can imagine.

Vence is his birthplace. It's called the City of Art, set on a hill near Nice overlooking the impossibly blue Mediterranean. There's an old town, a walled circle of Medieval buildings all packed together you have to see to believe.

From his ancestral villa, you look out over olive and orange trees, plus flowers of every description stretching to the sea. The soft air is filled with perfume. There's only one word to describe this part of the world. Exquisite.

Dominic's family owns the House of Eve. Their perfumeries process the precious oils from the flowers that grow on the hillsides. I learned today that this area of France is called "God's Garden." It's so beautiful here, it hurts.

You remember the Matisse print hanging in the living room, the one with the red background I bought? Well today I saw the Chappelle Matisse, the all-white chapel with stained-glass windows he designed and decorated. It's reputed to be his masterpiece. I can see why.

She was rambling again.

Dominic's mother has been vacationing at his sister's villa in Antibes. When he called to surprise her with the news that we had flown in to be married, she planned a party for tonight where I'll be meeting his family for the first time. I imagine they'll be as wonderful as his friends, Alik and Zane. Today they took us to lunch overlooking the water.

Her hand trembled, making it difficult to write. Was it only a week ago he'd come to her apartment demanding to know why she'd put the property up for sale? Now, unbelievably, it was the eve of their wedding. Dominic was the kind of man whose drive and resources allowed him to move at lightning speed to accomplish any objective.

Her eyes strayed to the antique canopied bed where a simple sleeveless black dress with a hem just above the knee lay on the eiderdown comforter. A gift from Dominic she couldn't refuse.

"Indulge me this once, *mon amour,*" he wrote on the card that accompanied the box a maid had delivered only moments ago.

She pressed the note to her heart. He'd been indulging her endlessly. Yesterday while several of the live-in maids fought to watch over Elizabeth, he'd taken Hannah shopping for a wedding dress. It was the kind of French haute couture salon where the *patronne* brought out several bridal creations she felt suitable for Hannah's height and figure. There were no price tags.

When she put on the floor-length white chiffon and lace with the capped sleeves and nipped-in waist, Dominic's eyes ignited like dark burning fires. Slowly his gaze traveled up her body to her face and hair before he nodded to the *patronne.*

Such an intimate look almost made Hannah's legs give way. Hot-faced from the memory, she hurriedly finished her letter.

After our honeymoon, which he's keeping a secret, we'll be living in Laramie.

Dominic is looking forward to meeting you and Steve. He hopes we can plan a reception to celebrate both our weddings.

In the meantime, he asked me to enclose this check to you for your half of the property.

It was too generous a sum, more than twice the amount she and Lisa might have gotten from the sale of the land had they waited for the best offer.

When she said as much to Dominic and intimated she would tear it up if he didn't take it back, his jaw hardened. He reminded her the money not only represented the property, but Lisa's willingness to let Hannah be Elizabeth's mother. She was a pearl beyond price. Under normal circumstances, he would have paid any sum to adopt her. If Hannah refused to send the check with her letter, then he would have it mailed under separate cover.

At that point Hannah didn't say another word. Her love for this incredibly unselfish man just kept growing.

I've given him my half as a wedding present. He wants to build a house on it.

At least that was what he was saying right now. Fear seized her heart because Hannah was convinced it would never come to pass. Say what you like, the opulence of the life he'd been born to went to make up part of what he was.

One day his bullet train will run through the backyard.

That was the only event Hannah could guarantee.

But as I told you at the beginning of this letter, I still have trouble believing any of this is real.

Take care of yourselves. I'll call you the minute we get back home.

All my love,
Hannah.

After folding everything in the overnight letter, she made out the label, then left it on the desk to be mailed while she hurried into the shower.

By the time she had emerged and had slipped into her new dress, Sophie, the sixty-ish maid who'd been with his mother the longest, came in from the adjoining room carrying Elizabeth. Dominic had put her in charge of the baby who seemed reasonably content as she reached for Hannah.

No doubt she'd been distracted by Sophie's infectious warmth, plus she was wearing a precious new pale pink dress with a scalloped hem and lace collar. On her feet she wore the whitest shoes and lace-trimmed stockings Hannah had ever seen. The baby kept grabbing at them. More of Dominic's generosity.

She imagined he'd shopped for everything personally. This wedding was the most important occasion of their lives, but when they settled down to married life, the gifts would have to stop. Elizabeth had already learned that all she had to do was look up at him with that worshipful expression, and he would move heaven and earth for her.

"Dominic says he will come for you and the little one in a moment," she explained in heavily accented English, clasping her hands together. "He calls the two of you his *anges*. We are so happy for you. A miracle happened since he went to live in America! I never thought to see Dominic this happy again."

Now would be the perfect time to ask questions about his past, but Hannah had never stooped to gossip, and refused to do so now.

"It's like a miracle for me, too," she responded, warmed by the other woman's words and her obvious adoration of Dominic.

"You love him very much. *C'est très bon, ca.*"

Hannah buried her face in the baby's neck. "Maybe too much," she murmured with tears in her voice.

"There's no such thing as too much love!" She threw her hands in the air. From what Hannah had seen since she'd been in France, it was a typical Gallic gesture.

"*Amen, ma douce.*"

Attuned to the sound of Dominic's voice, both Hannah's and Elizabeth's heads lifted in his direction at the same time. They lived for his attention. He would always be the center of their universe.

As he drew closer, his searching eyes fused with Hannah's. "Thank you for not putting on lipstick yet." Encircling them both in his arms, he lowered his mouth to hers. The savage hunger in his kiss left her light-headed and breathless. By the time he'd relinquished her trembling lips, her body gave a violent shake of unassuaged longing.

"I felt that," he whispered in an aching voice. "Don't you know I'm in the same kind of pain, *mon amour?*"

"Just remember that tomorrow is almost

here. After the ceremony, I'm spiriting you away where we'll be alone to concentrate on each other. I've been dreaming about it since the moment your angel eyes first looked down into mine. I promise you the pain will go away."

"Dominic—" she cried his name, too moved to talk because of the intensity of passion exploding between them.

"Tonight all you have to do is follow my lead."

Follow his lead?

Somehow those words sounded ominous as they passed through the tall French doors to the drawing room of the nineteenth-century villa. Right away Hannah spotted Dominic's father who was talking with a younger man.

At that precise moment, she felt Dominic tense before his arm unexpectedly tightened around her waist. Though he'd never talked about his father or mentioned that he might be here, she would know the senior Giraud anywhere.

Though not as tall as his son, the lean, handsome older man with strands of silver running through his dark hair carried himself with the same kind of male grace and sophistication he'd bequeathed to Dominic.

He'd dressed formally for the occasion in

an elegant navy pinstripe suit and tie, giving her an idea of how attractive Dominic would still be many years from now.

As Dominic guided her over the threshold with Elizabeth propped against his shoulder, Hannah heard a female voice cry his name. In the next breath, Dominic's mother flew across the room to embrace her son. Behind her raced his sister Nicole, as beautiful as Dominic was gorgeous in his own unequaled masculine way.

Hannah stepped back to allow the two women, both tall slender brunettes, to hug and kiss him, all the while making a fuss over Elizabeth who kept trying to hide her face in Dominic's neck.

In the background Hannah noticed his father staring at Dominic through hooded eyelids, but he didn't move from his position near the Louis XV love seat in ivory damask.

"It's so wonderful to see you, darling. Your marvelous news has kept me in tears ever since you phoned," his mother admitted before breaking down for another good cry.

Her British accent shouldn't have surprised Hannah. She knew his mother was English, but it sounded foreign in this French household. Having been raised bilingual from birth, no wonder Dominic spoke both languages perfectly.

"Mother— Nicole— I'd like you to meet the light of my life, Hannah Carr. And this little beauty is our daughter, Elizabeth."

Hannah had no idea how much his family knew about the situation with Elizabeth, but now wasn't the time to sort it out. For the next few minutes everything passed in a kind of blur as Hannah was hugged and kissed in genuine affection by both women who asked a dozen questions at once. Elizabeth was the star of the show, of course.

After prying the baby away from Dominic so they could get better acquainted with her, Dominic introduced Hannah to Nicole's husband, Jean-Jacques Armentier, who'd walked over to them.

Very attractive in his own right with a pair of intent, mischievous black eyes, he gave her a kiss on both cheeks.

"Welcome to the family, *cherie*. You really are the golden angel Dominic described. Now I have my answer."

"To what question?" Dominic sounded amused.

"When I heard the astounding news that your bachelor days were numbered, I said to myself, what is it about this American woman our French women haven't got? What has she done to cause Dominic to willingly exchange his freedom for a life of bondage?"

Nicole's husband was an obvious tease and had asked the questions in good fun. Unfortunately there was a discernible tremor in her voice when Hannah admitted, "I keep asking myself the same thing."

The expression on Jean-Jacques's face sobered. "You really don't know…" He darted a surprised-looking glance at Dominic. "You're a very lucky man, *mon vieux.*"

"I'm aware of that," Dominic murmured before pressing a hard kiss to her mouth. When he lifted his head, she realized Dominic's father had come to stand in front of them.

"Well, Dominic— It's been a long time. I guess I don't have to ask how you are."

When there was no physical gesture of affection between them, Hannah shrank inwardly.

"Father? You're looking well as ever. Please meet my bride-to-be, Hannah Carr."

"*Enchanté, Hannah.*" He raised her hand to his lips. "My son has exquisite taste."

"Thank you, *monsieur.*"

His gaze lingered on her face. "That's a

beautiful love child you two have created. I saw her earlier with Sophie."

Dominic stiffened and started to pull her away, but Hannah sent him a pleading look and remained where she was.

"Elizabeth is beautiful, but she's not our child."

He blinked. "No?"

"No. She's my niece, the daughter of my teenage sister. But the young man Lisa loved, ran off.

"Since she couldn't care for the baby herself, she decided to put Elizabeth up for adoption. At that point I told her I wanted to keep the baby, and she agreed. After Dominic and I are married, we're going to formally adopt her."

The older man looked stunned. "Is this true?" By now he'd leveled his dark eyes on his son.

"I'll have a DNA report sent to you," Dominic bit out, grim-faced.

A dull red crept into the older man's cheeks as he continued to stare at his son.

Aghast at the underlying bitterness between them, Hannah couldn't bear the tension any longer. It was too great a reminder of the heated battles between Lisa and their own father. To make matters worse, Hannah could hear the baby crying in the other room. She'd marveled that Elizabeth had lasted this long without needing to be rescued.

Dominic's arm slid around her shoulders. He kissed the side of her neck. "Shall we join the rest of the family?" This time she didn't resist when he ushered her away through another set of doors to a lavishly appointed dining room.

Obviously Elizabeth had become frightened by her strange surroundings. In her haste to get to her, Hannah scarcely had time to marvel at the palatial atmosphere replete with fresh flowers everywhere made up in their honor.

She and Dominic hurried over to his mother who'd been attempting to comfort the baby. Elizabeth caught sight of Dominic and did one of her flying leaps into his arms.

"Look at that!" Madame Giraud cried out, half laughing.

"The baby adores you, Dominic!" This from his sister.

Hannah had to admit he looked and acted every bit the proud father. His satisfied smile went a long way to push the tension of a minute ago to the background.

Once they were seated around the table with the baby happily ensconced against his chest, Hannah confided, "Elizabeth did that trick soon after she met Dominic. In fact she almost fell on the floor of my apartment in her eagerness to get to him.

"She's always been so shy around other people, particularly men, it was a shock to see how she behaved with Dominic, almost as if she chose him to be her father and no one else!"

Dominic smiled into the baby's golden hair. "It was a mutual love affair, wasn't it, *mignonne?*"

Nicole's brown eyes grew tender. "Tell us how you met my younger brother. We want details! Don't leave anything out!"

Hannah loved her at once. "Well—" she murmured, reading encouragement in Dominic's heart-stopping smile, "it began one night—"

"*Oh, non, mademoiselle.* First we must hear about this place you come from," Jean-Jacques interrupted her. "Laramie, Wyoming. Describe it for us."

"Compared to Vence, there is no comparison," she stated without hesitation. "This part of the Mediterranean is paradise." In fact she felt like she was in a dream with maids coming and going, serving them the most delicious food she'd ever tasted.

Dominic's hand slid to her thigh, sending heat through her body. "You're right, *mon amour*. But Laramie has its own unique brand of western beauty. You should see the little log cabin museum Hannah runs on her family's property. It's an old Pony Express way station surrounded by miles of prairie grass and Indian paintbrush."

"He forgot to tell you it's at seven thousand feet. The winters are very harsh, and the air is much thinner and dryer than the gorgeous climate here."

"You live so high?" Dominic's mother marveled.

"Yes. The land is fairly flat and unremarkable, except for the mountains, of course."

"And the sage," Dominic added. Looking into Hannah's eyes he murmured, "Perhaps you're used to the smell, but I will never be able to get enough of it."

For a man who'd grown up among the flowery fragrances of Provence, it pleased her he was sensitive to one of Wyoming's delights.

"Neither will I," she admitted quietly. To the others she explained, "When the earth gets baptized during a rainstorm, the sage seems to come alive. The air is so wonderfully clean and fragrant. That's when I love to get on my horse and take her for a gallop.''

She could hear Dominic breathe deeply. ''At first I thought Wyoming was a lonely place, but that was before I met Hannah. Now everything I could ever want is right there.''

Dominic should have been an actor. He had his family convinced there was no greater spot on earth, but Hannah happened to know differently.

''Tell us about your horse. What's its name?'' This from Nicole.

''Cinnamon.''

In front of everyone, Dominic removed his hand from her leg and placed it over her hand, squeezing gently. ''She's practically human.''

''How old were you when you learned to ride?''

''I don't know exactly. I think my mother put me on a horse when I was Elizabeth's age and taught me everything I know. She and my father both rode in the rodeo. That's how they met.''

''Are your parents still alive?''

''No. My mother died giving birth to my younger sister, Lisa, Elizabeth's birth mother. Years later my father developed a bad heart and worked for the postal service until he passed away.''

"Is your sister an expert rider like you?"

"She probably could have been, but my father went into depression after our mother died. I'm afraid he wasn't the most patient teacher. One day she announced she was never getting on another horse again, and that was it."

"Do you and Dominic ride together?"

He winked at Hannah. "We did once. It was the night she rescued me."

"Rescued you—" his mother cried. "Did you have an accident?" Everyone's eyes were alive with curiosity.

Dominic was loving this, but Hannah noticed he never addressed his father who sat silently at the other end of the table. The older Giraud watched them with unnerving concentration.

"Zane and Alik were right. I met my destiny when I overturned the Jeep on Hannah's property."

"Were you hurt?" both women blurted at the same time.

"I probably would have died if it hadn't been for my bride-to-be."

"That's not true!" Hannah challenged. "He's exaggerating," Without letting him say another word, she told his family exactly what happened that night.

"Hannah's being modest. She would have you think her errand of mercy was nothing, but I know otherwise." His voice grated.

"It was Cinnamon who was put through the paces." A flushed Hannah insisted on getting that part of the story right. "All I had to do was guide her and hold on to you so you wouldn't fall off."

"Ah..." Jean-Jacques smiled wickedly. "Now we're getting to the good part."

"You're wrong, *mon frère*. She sent me off to the hospital in an ambulance, refused any compensation for her trouble, and wouldn't give me the time of day for weeks! My only ally was this little cherub." He kissed the top of Elizabeth's head.

"Of course once Hannah is my wife, we'll ride double and she'll be the one sitting in front of me," came the silken assertion. Imagining that scenario sent Hannah's body into shock.

"Well, well—" Nicole's husband murmured. "The truth at last. You *literally* fell hard, *mon frère*." He threw his head back and laughed. "To think that after saving your life, she said *au revoir* to you. I believe Hannah is the only woman alive who ever told you to go away."

Nicole's smile lit her whole face. "It's a

very romantic story. But I still can't imagine how you managed to get my brother on your horse. You're an extraordinary woman.''

''It's in Hannah's genes,'' Dominic inserted. His hand had moved to the back of her neck where he massaged it gently. ''Her great-great-grandmother was a Pony Express rider.''

''Are you serious? A woman?'' Nicole questioned.

Hannah nodded. ''It's all there in her diary. She needed the money, and they wouldn't hire a woman to carry the mail. I still have the clothes she wore when she disguised herself as a man. Every summer I dress up like she did and ride in the Laramie parade.''

''Except for this year.'' Dominic bounced Elizabeth on his thigh. ''This year she had to miss it for our wedding.''

''Thank heaven for that! Thank *you* for helping him,'' Nicole said in a trembling voice. ''Dominic is very special to me.''

And to me, Nicole.

''To all of us!'' their mother chimed in.

Dominic lifted the baby in the air and kissed her tummy. ''When our house is built on Hannah's property, you and Jean-Jacques will have to fly over to Wyoming with the twins. We'll all go riding, even *Petite.*

"By the way, where are my rambunctious nephews? I was hoping to introduce them to their beautiful little cousin."

"They're getting over a cold," Dominic's mother answered him. "We thought it would be better to keep them away tonight so they wouldn't give it to Elizabeth."

Hannah smiled. "She just finished one before we came."

Nicole's lovely face glowed. "The boys are going to go crazy over her. I can't wait to watch their reactions when they all meet."

"We'll have to plan a big trip next year," her husband said. "Our sons will be old enough to enjoy your American Disneyland. Oh, yes, and Las Vegas. You must have been there many times, eh, Hannah?"

"Actually only once. My father lived on a fixed income." That was telling them about her situation with a vengeance. "We went on campouts and took the weekend trip to Denver and Omaha. After our father died, Lisa and I splurged.

"We flew to Southern California to see the ocean. It was our first ride on a plane. On the way back, we stopped in Las Vegas just to say we'd been there. I lost the package of dimes I bought playing the slot machines.

That was the extent of my career as a gambler.''

At that point both Jean-Jacques and Dominic broke into hearty laughter. When it subsided, Nicole's husband rose to his feet. He picked up his wineglass and stared down at Hannah.

"I'd like to propose a toast to my beautiful, courageous sister-to-be Hannah, and my brother, Dominic. May you be even happier at the end of your life together than you are right now."

"That's a perfect toast," said his mother.

Dominic's father followed suit by standing up. "I, too, wish you the joy of your marriage." He spoke before everyone else lifted their glasses.

Hannah noticed Dominic's hesitation before he swallowed the contents of his wineglass in one gulp. Then he pushed himself away from the table and helped Hannah to her feet. "It's past time our little princess was in bed."

"I—I've enjoyed every minute of this beautiful party." Hannah's voice caught. "You don't know how I've longed to meet all of you. Thank you for making me and the baby feel so welcome."

"It was our privilege," his mother assured

her as she got up from the table with the aid of her husband. "I've prayed the day would come when my son would find the right woman to complete his life. After meeting you and the baby, I realize that prayer has been answered."

"Thank you," Hannah whispered, deeply touched by her words.

The older woman's gray-blue eyes misted over before they traveled to her son. "You're very blessed, Dominic."

"I agree," came his husky response. "Hannah is my life! *Bonne nuit, la famille.*"

CHAPTER SEVEN

NICOLE was the last to say good-night before Dominic escorted Hannah to the nursery in the other wing of the villa.

Though the evening had gone so well, she sensed his dark thoughts where his father was concerned. She couldn't bear to see this brooding side of his nature.

Hopefully after they put the baby down, he would confide in her. Tomorrow was their wedding day. She didn't want the hint of a shadow to mar their happiness.

To her relief, Elizabeth fell asleep almost as soon as her head touched the crib mattress. It had been a huge day for her. Quietly they put out the light and tiptoed into Hannah's room.

She turned in his arms. "Darlin—"

"No postmortem's tonight." He stifled the endearment against her lips before devouring them.

It would be the easiest thing in the world to allow their passion to blot out the world.

But Hannah had been too disturbed by what she'd seen transpire between him and his father to let it go.

Finally she tore her lips from his, but his arms prevented her escape. "We *have* to talk, Dominic. Why are you and your father so estranged? If I'm going to be your wife, I need to know. Please help me understand," she begged.

His chest heaved. "I had hoped he wouldn't show up tonight. The last thing I wanted was for him to make you uncomfortable."

"But he didn't! Naturally he was curious about Elizabeth, and had a right to know if she was your baby."

Dominic's expression grew wintry. "No, Hannah." His hands ran the length of her arms before he let go of her. "My father's agenda was much less noble than that. But he hadn't counted on you being the kind of woman you are. The truth backfired on him."

"What do you mean? Did he expect me to lie?"

After a slight pause, "He didn't expect you to say anything at all. What he wanted was a confrontation with me."

"Why?"

While she waited for his answer, she sank down on the edge of the bed.

He raked a bronzed hand through his hair. "My father has always been a renowned womanizer, not exactly a boy's best role model."

Hannah moaned.

"Though he's had numerous affairs, mother never divorced him. But they've lived separate lives even when they've been together, if you know what I mean."

She nodded, stunned by the revelation. Not because his story was so different than that of millions of estranged couples in the world. It just seemed sad to think that people from such a unique background and heritage, people who appeared to have everything to make their world perfect, still managed to destroy their lives and those of their children.

"It's very tragic."

"It *was* tragic growing up because I loved them both. But when I matured enough to understand my mother's pain, I lost respect for my father and told him exactly what I thought of him.

"He cautioned me that no man is perfect, that one day I might find myself in the same position. I informed him he was wrong, that if I were ever fortunate enough to fall in love with a woman as wonderful as my mother, I would remain faithful to her. From that point on I distanced myself from him.

"This grieved mother because no matter what, she has loved him to this day and has fought to keep the family together. He claims that she's the only women he ever loved, though his actions certainly haven't proved it.

"Naturally he expected me, his only son, to help run the family perfume business which began several hundred years ago. From my birth I was groomed to take over for him one day. But by the time I'd reached my early twenties, I couldn't tolerate his behavior no matter how discreetly he thought he handled his affairs.

"In the end I made a compromise with my mother. I told her I would be willing to run the New York end of the business, and come home for vacations and holidays."

Finally Hannah understood why he lived in America.

"On one of my return trips to New York, I stopped off in England to sit in on a seminar of engineers and scientists who'd worked on the Eurotunnel project across the English Channel. It was there I met up with Alik and Zane who were also in attendance from the States. Our eventual partnership made the bonds of friendship even stronger, and changed the course of my life.

"I informed my parents I was stepping down from my position with the company to concentrate fully on the bullet train project. Mother begged me not to cut off everything with my father, so I agreed to be available for consulting."

Hannah got up from the bed. "He must be in even greater shock to realize you're planning to stay in America and marry a woman with a child who's not even yours."

"He *wishes* Elizabeth were mine. That way he could accuse me of sowing my own version of wild oats. He has a weakness for other women, but he's only reminded of it when I'm around.

"The truth is, he was hoping ours wasn't a love match, *mon amour*. Nothing would please him more than to believe you're one of those predatory females who got pregnant with my child to trap me into marrying you. Then he could gloat over my lack of judgment and watch me turn to other women behind your back."

"That's horrible!" She buried her face in her hands.

In the next breath she felt arms of whipcord draw her against his body until she was molded to him. "Perhaps it was best we got that out of the way. Now we never have to discuss my father again, and there are no secrets between us."

Her luminous green eyes lifted to his. "No, darling. None."

He covered her face and mouth with hungry kisses. "*Mon Dieu!* I've never wanted or needed you as badly as I do at this moment." He pressed his forehead against hers.

"The selfish part of me doesn't want to wait until tomorrow to make you my wife in every sense of the word. But the other part says that in a little over twelve hours, we'll be ensured days and nights of uninterrupted privacy to really love each other the way nature intended. Tell me to leave, Hannah," he implored. "Help me do the right thing—"

Immune to his entreaty, her arms tightened around his waist in the feverish need to meld with him. "What if I don't wan—"

But she was prevented from saying anything else because Sophie unexpectedly appeared in the doorway carrying an inconsolable Elizabeth in her arms.

"*Je m'excuse,* but the *bébé*— She woke up and couldn't find you."

"It's all right, Sophie. Come here to me, petite."

After a hard kiss to Hannah's mouth, he crossed the room to lift Elizabeth from the other woman's arms. "*Merci,* Sophie. I'll put her back to bed when she's ready."

The maid beamed. "Already she has stopped crying now that she is with her *papa!*"

While she slipped away, Hannah stood there in a stupor-like condition. She'd been so on fire for Dominic, she'd lost all cognizance of her surroundings, even the baby's tears.

A wry smile broke out on Dominic's handsome face. "It seems Elizabeth is my little guardian angel. She heard my cry for help, and came to my rescue in time to make certain her mommy stays as pure as that white confection she's going to wear tomorrow."

He lifted his dark head and stared hard into Hannah's eyes. "I can't wait to see you in it again when we stand before the priest. You took my breath the night you found me by the river. I've never been the same since."

"Neither have I," she blurted emotionally. "If babies could speak, Elizabeth would tell you exactly what I confided to her after the paramedics took you away."

"Am I going to have to wait until she's

old enough to express herself before I hear the details?'' he whispered provocatively.

There was this suffocating feeling in her chest. ''Only until tomorrow night.''

''Be warned I plan to hold you to that,'' came his fierce avowal. ''Now, for what's left of this one, Elizabeth and I will let you catch up on your beauty sleep.'' His eyes flashed dark fire. ''You're going to need it.''

Dominic held the baby while she finished her bottle, but she still hadn't closed her eyes. He smoothed her delicate brows with his thumb, marveling at each sweet feature of a face that reminded him of Hannah.

''You know something earthshaking is going to happen tomorrow, don't you, *Petite*. That's why you're still awake.

''Much as I hate to be separated from you, your mother and I need time alone together after we're married. I never expected to fall in love like this. Will you forgive me if I want to keep her to myself for a week? The way I feel about her, seven days sailing the Mediterranean won't be nearly long enough. But in that short amount of time we'll both be missing you too much, and we'll hurry back.

''Don't forget that while we're gone, your

grand-mère and Tante Nicole are going to dote on you, and you'll learn to love them. By the time we return from our honeymoon, I suspect you'll be fast friends with Etienne and Pierre. That's good because I want the three of you to become very close."

He kissed her nose. "I wonder where your pacifier is. Something tells me it will help you to sleep. Let's see if we can find it."

Propping her against his shoulder, he got up from the chair and went over to the armoire for the diaper bag. He remembered Hannah packing it with some of Elizabeth's toys.

Three of the compartments had been emptied. He unzipped the fourth and found what he was looking for wedged between the pages of what he presumed was a baby magazine. No doubt she'd forgotten she'd stashed it there.

Instead of an icy cold shower, maybe he ought to read the latest parenting tips to keep his mind off his bride-to-be. She was as close as the other side of the wall. If he joined her, he knew she wouldn't refuse him.

Taking a fortifying breath, he pulled both items from the bag and tossed the magazine on the double bed next to the crib. "It's time to go to sleep now, *mignonne*."

He put the pacifier in Elizabeth's mouth and lay her down. After covering her with a light blanket, he sat on the edge of the bed where she could still see him through the bars.

A smile broke the corner of his mouth. Her eyelids were getting heavier and kept fluttering. In a few seconds they'd be closed. While he waited, he reached for the magazine.

U.S. Economics. "Meet America's 289 Billionaires."

That despised article with unauthorized photographs taken by the bloodthirsty paparazzi.

Bile rose in his throat.

He hadn't known about any of it until it was too late to stop the press. If he'd sued the magazine, some damn tabloid reporter would have got wind of it and created another media frenzy with more atrocious publicity, the last thing he wanted for himself or his family.

Nothing was sacred.

He got to his feet ready to destroy it. Then realization dawned.

Hannah had known who he was from the beginning…

* * *

"Dom?"

"I heard the tender bring you alongside. I'm glad you're here. Come in and shut the door."

Through veiled eyes Dominic watched Alik and Zane enter the study of the yacht he'd had prepared for his honeymoon. Everything and anything he could think of to make her happy.

Hannah hadn't led the easiest life. He wanted to make up for every deprivation, take away every pain. Love her till the end of time.

"Sit down, *mes camarades*."

Both men remained standing. Alik spoke first. "What's going on, Dom? When we asked if we could give you a bachelor party, you said you didn't want to spend your last night away from home."

Dominic took another swallow of champagne, the best vintage from his family's private wine cellar.

"I stayed with Elizabeth until she fell asleep. When it became apparent she wasn't going to wake up, I decided to take advantage of my last night of freedom."

Zane shook his head. "You're the one groom I know who doesn't have cold feet. So tell us how come you've suddenly felt the need to throw your own party at two o'clock in the morning and wake us out of a much needed sleep?''

"More to the point, you're being married in a little less than nine hours," Alik reminded him. "What is the matter with you?" His eyes stared pointedly at the glass in Dominic's hand.

"I'm not drunk if that's what you're worried about. In fact this is my first glass, although I thought that drinking was part of what a bachelor party was all about," he mocked Alik who was starting to irritate him. They both were.

Zane pulled up a chair, then straddled it. "Dom— This must have to do with your father. He said or did something unforgivable tonight.''

"Did he hurt Hannah?" Alik demanded quietly.

Dominic twirled the stem of the empty champagne glass in his fingers. "All of the above. But I'd rather not discuss him."

Mon Dieu! All I want is for the pain to stop.

"Here. I put out two glasses for you. In case you didn't know, I've been saving this particular bottle for a very special occasion."

"Conserve the rest until Hannah's on board so she can enjoy it with you."

"No. This is for my friends." His gaze took in the two of them. "You've never let me down."

"For the love of God," Zane muttered, his brows meeting in a frown, "out with it, man! Tell us what's eating you alive."

Dominic set his champagne glass on the table. The taste had turned bitter. He was beginning to wish he hadn't phoned them, after all. In an economy of movement he levered himself from the chair and went to stand by the window where he could see the harbor.

"It doesn't really matter now. The deed's been done. I thought you guys might enjoy seeing Nice from the water at night. It's one of the world's most photographed sights."

"Good Lord, Dom. It's Hannah who's turned you inside out. I recognize the signs."

Something twisted in Dominic's gut just hearing her name. "I don't want to talk about her right now, Alik."

"After what Blaire did to me, you think I don't understand?" Alik bit out. "But Hannah's not Blaire. The woman's deeply in love with you. What you two have is so rare, you need to grab it and hold on with both hands. Every man should be so lucky." His voice grated.

As if he'd come up against a wall of flame,

Dominic spun away from the view. "Is *that* what you call it," came the sarcastic retort.

After a tension-filled silence, "So there's not going to be a wedding and you wanted us to be the first to know, is that it?" This from Zane.

Dominic's eyes glittered dangerously. "No. Everything will proceed as planned."

Zane eyed him boldly. "If you're feeling like this, then you have no business getting married."

"The baby loves and needs me. I happen to know *her* feelings are a hundred percent genuine. That's reason enough."

"The hell it is!" they both exclaimed at the same time.

"Postpone the wedding a few days until you can get your head on straight. Everyone will understand if you and Hannah need a little more private time together to talk this out."

"Zane's right. Whatever you imagin—"

"This has nothing to do with imagination," Dominic cut him off icily. "No matter how much you're still hurting over the brutal way Blaire ended your engagement, at least she had the guts to be honest with you. In the end that's all that matters."

Both men stared at him with generous amounts of anxiety and compassion.

"Is there another man?"

Zane's ironic question caused him to suck in his breath. "No. Nothing so simple…

"Mon Dieu!" he moaned the words aloud. "I'm not fit company for anyone tonight. Forgive me for dragging you out here. Go ahead and take the tender back to the port. I'll call for a car to run you to your hotel."

"If you think we're going to leave you like this—" Alik muttered.

"Don't worry. I've learned the hard way alcohol can't solve what's wrong with me," he said in a grim tone as he tore off his T-shirt. "If you'll excuse me, I'm going for a swim."

"Sounds good to us. We'll join you."

"I'm not talking about a dip in the deck pool."

Zane's lips tightened. "We didn't think you were."

"Ah, mademoiselle!" one of the younger maids cried out when she saw Hannah in her wedding finery. "You look like an angel, all white and gold. Monsieur Dominic will be speechless when he sees you."

"Thank you for those kind words."

Hannah's heart pounded too hard. It didn't seem possible that her wedding day was here at last. In less than an hour she was going to marry the man she loved heart and soul.

"There's a car out in front waiting for you."

After adjusting her veil in front of the mirror, Hannah turned to the maid. "Do you know where Dominic is?"

"He already left for the church with Monsieur *et* Madame Giraud."

Hannah swallowed her disappointment and looked away, hoping the maid wouldn't notice her distress. Perhaps his mother was a stickler about it being bad luck to see the bride before the wedding.

But the Dominic Hannah loved moved through life according to his own set of rules, no one else's. If he'd wanted to see her this morning, tradition wouldn't have kept him away. Hannah had been waiting breathlessly for him.

"Is there anything I can help you with before you leave, *mademoiselle?*"

Feeling unaccountably bereft, Hannah had forgotten the maid was still standing there. She lifted her head.

"No, thank you. I'll just say goodbye to the baby one more time, then go down."

"The *bébé* isn't in her room, *mademoiselle*. After you finished playing with her earlier this morning, Monsieur Dominic took her out to the garden. She's still there with Sophie, very content."

"I see." But Hannah didn't see at all. Disappointment changed to bewilderment because he hadn't even come in to say good morning or steal a kiss. It would have been the natural thing to do, seeing as the baby was in the adjoining room.

"Are you all right, *mademoiselle?*"

"I—I think I have a case of pre-wedding nerves," she dissembled.

The maid looked perplexed. "But how could you? He's such a magnificent man! Don't you realize every woman in France wishes she were the one marrying Monsieur Dominic today?" Her hands flew in the air. "So many have tried to capture his heart. *Tant pis* for them. I have seen him watching you. He doesn't know anyone else exists."

"Thank you for saying that," Hannah whispered, touched by the maid's attempt to be of comfort.

Right now Hannah craved reassurance. She wished her mother were still alive. A bride needed her own family around.

It saddened her that neither she nor Lisa

could be there for each other on their wedding days. Unfortunately the situation with Elizabeth had been of too delicate a nature.

But since everything was resolved on that score, Hannah determined to get closer to her sister. She hoped the letter she'd sent would smooth the way for a new beginning for them.

"Mademoiselle?" the maid prompted, looking a little anxious.

"I'm ready." With the plain gold wedding band she'd bought for Dominic wrapped inside the lace handkerchief clutched in her hand, she followed the maid through the villa to the front entrance. A dashing Jean-Jacques, dressed in a dark blue silk suit with a rose in the lapel, stood in the circular drive waiting for her.

"At last! You look like a lovely floating cloud, but I must admit I was ready to come in and find you. Dominic will have my head if we arrive late. The ceremony is scheduled to start at eleven o'clock. We have ten minutes."

"I'm sorry. I'll tell him it was all my fault."

"Don't apologize. It's tradition for the bride to arrive after the groom. Besides it's good for Dominic to think you're not as eager. Let him worry a little longer about whether *you* are going to make it," he teased. "It adds to the excitement."

A gentle laugh escaped her throat. Jean-Jacques was exactly the medicine she needed.

Relieved that Nicole's husband had remained behind to drive her to the church, she allowed him to help her get in the back seat of the black luxury estate car. It was the same kind of car Dominic had been driving when some photographer had taken his picture.

After Jean-Jacques had arranged her gown to keep it protected, he shut the door and hurried around to the driver's seat.

The second they drove through the private gate leading to the villa they were bombarded by reporters and journalists. Almost blinded by so many flashes of light, Hannah lowered her head.

From the front seat she could hear colorful French pouring from Jean-Jacque's lips, reminding her of Dominic. "I'm sorry, Hannah," he apologized once they turned the corner and sped away.

"Somehow the paparazzi always know when Dominic returns home. He chose an obscure church for the ceremony and arranged for tight security, but don't be surprised when pictures of you make the front page of *France*

Soir and the *Figaro*. He's more popular than any eligible crown prince living in Europe today."

His comments underlined what the maid had said to her a few minutes ago. "No doubt they'll report that Elizabeth is the result of our anticipating our wedding vows."

He nodded, confirming her worst fears. "It's good you understand. My advice is stay away from anything to do with the media."

"You mean I might not like headlines that read, 'French perfume king lowers his sights to marry hick American rodeo queen?' Don't worry, I won't read or look at anything to do with the news." Her voice trembled.

Only now was it beginning to dawn on her she was marrying a real celebrity, though she knew Dominic never thought of himself in that light. How difficult his life must have been in that regard.

"You're the woman he loves," Jean-Jacques muttered sincerely, "and now that I'm getting to know you, I love you, too. Just remember that nothing else matters except your feelings for each other."

Jean-Jacques was very sweet. "Thank you for reminding me."

"You and I have a lot in common, *ma chère*. I was an unimportant chemist hired by the Giraud company who happened to fall in love with Nicole. Miraculously she returned my love and proposed to me.''

"You're kidding!"

"No!'' He shook his head emphatically. "Ask anyone in the family and they will tell you. She was like the princess on the glass hill. I was afraid to get on my horse and ride up to her.''

"I know exactly what you mean,'' she admitted in a quiet tone.

"Because she's Dominic's beautiful sister, and a Giraud at the same time, she is, and always will be, a celebrity in her own right, hounded by the press. But in spite of them, we've managed to be private most of the time and enjoy our children. You and Dominic will find a way to do the same.''

"I love you for sharing something so intimate with me. You don't know how much I needed to hear it.''

"Any time,'' he muttered as they were waved on past a barricade of police holding back a flank of reporters taking more pictures.

Up a winding street they drove toward a tiny, ancient-looking church almost hidden by other buildings of Medieval design. Only a few cars were parked on either side of the road.

"Eh, bien, there is your groom looking fierce and impatient. I do believe we gave him a scare. *Dieu merci,* I have delivered his bride in one piece."

Hannah had already spotted Dominic outside the church, tall, dark and resplendent in a formal black suit with two yellow roses attached to the lapel. He was such a gorgeous man that for a minute she couldn't do anything but stare at him in awe while she waited for her heart to resume its normal beat.

He moved off the step into the strong sunlight and strode toward the car. To her astonishment, once the door was open he climbed part way inside and kissed her on the mouth with almost primitive hunger.

"Easy, *mon frère,"* Jean-Jacques chided in a playful tone from the front seat. "You're not supposed to do that until the honeymoon starts."

When Dominic finally relinquished her mouth, the beautiful brown eyes she loved were shuttered, making it impossible to read their expression.

Hannah was still trying to recover from the sheer sensuality of that kiss when he said, "It's *my* wedding, Jean-Jacques. I can do what I want on this day of all days."

With that effortless male grace which was

an integral part of him, he helped her from the car.

"Are you ready, *mon amour?* The priest is waiting to bind us together as one flesh. For better or for worse, until death do us part."

Jean-Jacques had come around to her other side. "Whew. Dominic is very tense this morning," he whispered against her hot cheek. "We really did give him a fright, but *pas de problème.* It will make him appreciate you that much more. Just keep smiling. He'll eventually get over it. Pre-wedding jitters come to every groom, even someone as seemingly invincible as my brother-in-law."

Though Jean-Jacques was making light of Dominic's behavior, Hannah had the presentiment that something else was wrong with her husband-to-be.

Something had happened to him since he'd left her bedroom last night. It was traumatic enough to have gone soul-deep.

With a strange sense of foreboding rather than joy, she grasped his outstretched hand. Together they entered the tiny, Romanesque church.

Dominic's mother came right up to Hannah with a smile before presenting her with a bouquet of orange blossoms and yellow roses. "Be happy, my dear."

"I am," Hannah whispered emotionally, acknowledging the fragrant gift with a kiss on both cheeks. But inside she was shaking.

If the frescoes were beautiful, she didn't notice. The presence of his family and friends, Alik and Zane, seated in the tiny church, barely registered as Dominic led her to the front of the chapel where the priest awaited them.

If she could, she would have run back outside and demanded that Dominic tell her what was wrong, but he'd put a strong arm around her waist and gave her no opening. Then it was too late because the priest had started the ceremony.

"Dearly Beloved, we have gathered together in this sacred place to honor two wonderful people who have chosen to participate in the greatest sacrament of the church, that of holy matrimony. Let us pray."

Hannah bowed her head. While she prayed for the man who was about to become her husband, she shivered so hard the white chiffon rippled from the scooped neckline of her wedding dress to the lace dusting the stone floor.

Much of the ceremony passed by in a blur. She must have responded at the proper times.

To her intense relief Dominic's voice sounded strong and sure as he made his vows.

As the priest pronounced them man and wife, and instructed them to exchange rings, Dominic lifted her veil and embraced her with the same loving, tender passion he'd exhibited throughout their courtship.

Suddenly she felt everything was going to be all right. By the time they'd signed the marriage documents and she had accepted everyone's congratulations including kisses from Alik and Zane, Hannah decided they'd both been attacked by wedding nerves, nothing else.

A wave of longing passed through her body when Dominic pulled her away from his buddies and gave her a husbandly kiss on the mouth. "Come with me, Mrs. Giraud. Jean-Jacques is waiting to drive us back to the house to change."

"I'm ready," she whispered feverishly against his lips. "Now that I'm your wife, can't you tell me where we're going on our honeymoon?"

His dark eyes gleamed mysteriously. "All in good time."

CHAPTER EIGHT

"MADAME GIRAUD? I'm Michel Patrou, your pilot for this trip."

"It's very nice to meet you, Michel."

"Congratulations on your wedding. I hope you and Dominic will find great happiness together. Your husband told me to tell you he will join you in a minute. Then we will take off. What can I do to make you more comfortable?"

"I'm fine, thank you. Dominic already gave me this lemonade to drink."

"*Bon.* Then I will leave you to your privacy. As soon as your husband is back on board, we'll be taking off."

Hannah looked around the elegant interior of Dominic's company jet. To avoid the press, they'd flown to Nice from Vence in his company's helicopter, then boarded the plane.

She could hardly credit that any of this was happening. Dressed in a chic white linen designer suit with a chiffon scarf in blues and greens he'd insisted on giving her for a going away present, Hannah felt like a pampered princess.

Dominic had already done so much for her, she didn't want any more presents. The only thing she craved was to be alone with him. She hoped their honeymoon destination wasn't far from here. For too long she'd dreamed of making love with him. The physical wanting had turned to pain. He'd promised to take it away...

"Hannah?"

As soon as she heard his vibrant male voice, she leaped from the seat to run into his arms. But she came to a standstill when she saw him enter the plane carrying the baby against his cream silk sport shirt.

Her heart plunged to her feet. "Elizabeth!" she cried out in panic. "What's wrong with her, Dominic?"

"Not a thing," he said in a mild voice. "I'm afraid *I'm* the one with the problem."

Her delicately arched brows formed a frown of bewilderment. "What do you mean?"

"While she and I were playing in the garden this morning, I discovered that I would miss her too much to leave her behind, so I arranged for her to be brought to the airport.

Would you mind holding her while I get the rest of her things put on board?''

He handed her the baby before disappearing. Immediately Elizabeth started to cry as was her usual reaction when Dominic left her. But for once, shock made Hannah slow to respond to the baby's needs.

Like a revelation it came to her that Dominic's performance throughout the wedding ceremony had been solely for the benefit of their guests.

Her instincts had been right, after all. Whatever was wrong with Dominic had scarred his soul. Otherwise he could never have been this cruel to her. Not on their wedding day.

She refused to look at him as he stowed the baby's paraphernalia on board. But all Elizabeth had to do was see him to start fussing and want out of Hannah's arms.

Needing to channel the hurt and anger with something physical, she got up and deposited the baby in his lap without saying anything.

He grasped her wrist before she could turn away. ''You were eager to know before. Now that we're alone, aren't you going to ask me where I'm taking you?''

His mockery was so foreign, she was

wounded all over again by the dramatic change in him.

"Since there's obviously not going to be a honeymoon, it's a moot point. Unless everything has been a lie, something happened to kill your love for me after you left my bedroom last night.

"What I don't understand is how you could have derived any satisfaction from luring me to the altar when you feel this kind of enmity toward me."

Damn. Her eyes had filled with tears. "Why did you make us go through the motions when you could have called off the wedding before we left for the church this morning?"

His silence enraged her.

"You pursued me, remember?" Her proud chin lifted.

"Then suddenly before God, your family and your best friends, you made a mockery of my love for you." Her voice shook, causing her chest to heave.

His gaze swept over her body with stunning male intimacy. "You'd better sit down," he warned quietly. "We're ready to take off."

She could tell Elizabeth had sensed the tension and didn't know whether to smile or cry.

Her soulful eyes followed Hannah to her seat. No sooner had she strapped herself in than the jet taxied down the runway.

Within minutes they were airborne.

Hannah glanced out the window, watching the blue Mediterranean recede. She'd been given a brief glimpse of paradise, only to have it snatched away, forever out of reach. By the time they'd reached cruising speed, Elizabeth had fallen asleep.

Dominic put her in the infant seat, then poured himself a drink from the mini bar.

Unable to stand it any longer she asked, "How long do you plan to punish me without telling me what I've done? My father could be cruel like that, but I never would have suspected such behavior from you."

"Apparently we were both fooled." He tossed his drink back in one swallow.

Hannah didn't think her heart was in big enough pieces to break again. "About what? I don't understand."

His features looked chiseled. "How long did you plan to live with me before you admitted that you knew exactly who I was when you found me by the river?"

"But I didn't!"

"Don't lie to me, Hannah," he ground out. "I found the evidence in the diaper bag."

She shook her head in exasperation. "What are you talking about?"

In an economy of movement he reached for it and unzipped one of the compartments. Out came the issue of U.S. Economics.

"So *that's* where it was..." she cried the second she saw it. "I remember now. I'd taken it the pediatrician's office to read while I waited for the doctor to examine Elizabeth."

He stared down at her with an expression as bleak as the land around the museum in the dead of winter. "This issue came out fourteen months before we met."

"But I didn't see *it* or those pictures of you inside until I was sitting in Jim Thornton's garage getting my car safety inspected the week after you took me to dinner. If you'll look on the back outside page, you'll notice the sticker with his name and address on it."

But she could see Dominic was too incensed to look at anything.

"I asked him if I could buy it because...because I knew you would eventually be moving on, and I wanted a souvenir of you," she admitted in a small voice.

His body stood like one of those trees in the petrified forest.

"If you want to know the whole truth, after

Jim gave it to me, I carried it with me every place I went so I could always feast my eyes on you. I even took it with me to the pediatrician's office the night Elizabeth got sick.

"In my haste to buy her a steamer and get her home to bed, I put it in the diaper bag and then forgot about it because you were waiting for me at the apartment when I got home. After that I didn't need to keep looking at it because I had the real thing to hold on to and adore."

No matter what she said, he wasn't listening.

"Dominic— I never dreamed you would propose to me. From the start I feared you would go away for good, so I had this plan that one day I would hang that picture in the museum after your bullet train was built.

"Then I could point to it in my old age and say, 'See that man? I once knew him and h-have always loved him,'" she stammered. "'The bullet train that whizzes across this land was his dream,'" came her soulful confession.

His eyes narrowed in disdain. "You need to get your stories straight. You can't very well hang the picture of your beloved in the museum and point to it in your old age if you were planning to get rid of the property."

She shivered from his cruel mockery. This was worse than any nightmare. "No, of course not. That was before Lisa told me I could adopt Elizabeth, and we decided to sell the land."

"You mean before you found someone who you knew could meet your price," he inserted with a bitter twist of his lips. "*Mon Dieu!* You *had* to know I had fallen so hard for you, you could squeeze as much cash out of me as you wanted without even trying." He flayed her with crushing derision.

She shook her head in abject despair. "That's not true. Darling—when I brought you in from the river on Cinnamon, I had no idea who you were.

"But I began to suspect something when that waitress asked for your autograph. I sensed how much you hated being bothered by her. You reacted like someone who has had to put up with people like that for years.

"It wasn't until after I saw that article and found out your family owned the House of Eve that I understood *why* you kept quiet about your background.

"I suppose I could have told you the truth that night. But I decided not to say anything because I didn't want to be like all the other people in the world who must crowd around you and hound you to death for favors. I can't imagine anything worse than everyone wanting a piece of you." Her voice shook.

"You have to understand I had no illusions that you could love me. I thought I was a nobody. I still think so…"

In the silence that followed, lines darkened his face. She didn't know he could look that remote. Nothing she'd said had gotten through to him.

"When I received that call from the Realtor," he began in a gravelly voice, "I flew back to Laramie believing that you couldn't let me go because you recognized that what we shared was rare… beyond price."

"It *is*. I love you, Dominic!" she cried from the depths of her being. "I married you today because you're my whole life!" Adrenaline drove her to her feet.

His dark eyes glittered dangerously as he tossed the magazine on the table. The noise wakened the baby who started to cry, but for once Hannah could tell he was too far gone to deal with her.

"Until I saw that magazine last night, you had me totally fooled, Hannah Carr. The golden-haired angel who promised paradise with one flash of her impossibly green eyes.

The boots should have warned me she was part mortal and therefore as corruptible as the next person."

"*Dominic!*" she cried in anguish. "You don't really mean that!"

She saw him glance toward the cockpit. In a bold move, she raced past him and blocked the door.

"Get out of my way, Hannah." His mouth looked white around the edges.

"You'll have to make me, and I know some moves," she dared him.

French invective flowed from his lips. "It's not good to let Elizabeth go on screaming like that."

"Along with my other sins, are you now accusing me of being a bad mother?"

More untranslatable epithets escaped.

"How can I prove to you that I love you, that your money never meant anything to me?" Her whole body was trembling now, even her voice.

"I noticed you sent my check to your sister."

"Because you insisted!"

He smirked. "You knew I would."

"Dominic, darling— Please don't be like this."

"I think you'd better pick up the baby. She's becoming hysterical."

"What are you going to do? Sit with the pilot for the rest of the trip to Denver?"

"I'm glad you realize we're not stopping off in New York to stay at my penthouse. As I recall that's where you wanted to live, but you're not going to be granted that wish."

"Such a comment isn't worthy of you, Dominic. Please don't open that door. Michel will know something's wrong, and he was so kind to me before we took off."

"I'll tell him the baby's sick and she only wants her *maman*."

By now Hannah was so convulsed, she could hardly see him through the tears. "Does this mean you're asking me for a divorce?"

"No," came the emphatic response. "I would never give my father the satisfaction. As for Elizabeth, I love her and intend to be her father in every sense of the word."

Hannah gasped. "But you don't love *me* anymore."

"Since when is that a problem? My parents have managed to remain married and still live separate lives. I suspect we can do the same."

She was out of her mind with grief. "I

won't live with you under those circumstances.''

He darted her an accusatory glance. ''A minute ago you professed to love me. Apparently my mother is one of a dying breed. Enjoy the trip, *mon amour*. There's plenty of food and drinks in the galley for you and the baby.''

''Wake up, Hannah. We've landed. Your car's outside.''

She stirred, then looked at Dominic through puffy eyelids. He was bouncing Elizabeth against his shoulder.

Her nightmare hadn't gone away. A sharp, stabbing pain had started up in her heart again.

The last thing she recalled was him deserting her. After she'd fed the baby a bottle to settle her down, Hannah had cried for hours. Exhaustion from her wedding day and the traumatic aftermath must have finally taken over. She couldn't believe they were in Colorado already.

Her linen dress had ridden up her thighs, exposing her silky legs to his perusal. Quickly she got to her feet, then moaned because her clothes were a mass of wrinkles.

She didn't need a mirror to imagine how bad she looked.

Dominic must have taken their luggage to the car. He seemed impatient to be off. She hurried into the bathroom to freshen up, then left the plane.

The warm, muggy, late July evening was typical for Denver. She looked around to say goodbye to the pilot and thank him for the safe trip, but he was nowhere to be found.

Without any words passing between them, Dominic held the passenger door open for her. His dark, handsome features made her breath catch before she climbed in. He wasn't just any man taking her home. He was her husband. Tonight was their wedding night.

Surely by now he'd gotten past his anger enough to look forward to making love. She'd been living for it...

"There's the exit for Fort Collins," he murmured forty-five minutes later. Finally he'd broken the deathly silence. "We could stop and visit your sister."

If he'd made the suggestion with the idea of dashing her hopes for a bridal night of unleashed passion, then he'd more than accomplished his objective.

"My letter won't even reach her until tomorrow. I'd prefer it if she didn't know we didn't go on a honeymoon after all. Like you, I don't want my family to learn my marriage failed before it ever began.''

"Touché."

The last time they'd driven the hour-long stretch between Fort Collins and Laramie, her heart had cried inwardly because she didn't believe Dominic would ever love her.

Tonight her heart lay in splinters because *she knew he didn't.*

It was providential the baby was too young to understand what was going on. But one day Elizabeth would grow up and start asking questions. When that time came, Hannah couldn't imagine that she and Dominic would still be living like his parents.

To stay in a loveless marriage was anathema to her. But so was the thought of not having Dominic in her life at all.

She'd fought a valiant fight against breaking down in front of him, but the minute he drove into the parking space of her apartment, she jumped out of the passenger side and opened the back door to get the baby.

''Come on, sweetheart. Let's take you inside.'' She pulled Elizabeth from her car seat and carried her up the stairs, leaving Dominic to bring in everything else.

Laramie must have been experiencing

cooler weather. The apartment felt pleasant as she unlocked the door and headed for the baby's bedroom. "Here we are, back home safe and sound."

Elizabeth acted happy to be in her crib. Within a few minutes Hannah had changed into shorts and blouse to give her a bath. Now she was ready for bed.

Hannah carried her into the kitchen where Dominic had been emptying the diaper bag of baby bottles and extra canned formula. She wondered if the day would ever come when she didn't react to the sight of his virile male physique like some lovesick teenager.

"Elizabeth wants to say goodnight to her daddy. I'll finish up in here."

Dominic washed his hands, then reached for her. "Hmm. You smell divine, *mignonne*. I have a bottle ready for you." His tenderness with Elizabeth was all that sustained Hannah.

For fear of going to pieces, she worked around the apartment emptying her bags and putting toiletries away. When that was done, she made an omelette and coffee for Dominic, knowing he must be hungry for some hot food.

She met him coming out of the nursery. Her first instinct was to throw herself in his arms and never let him go, but of course she couldn't do that. Forcing herself to back away from him she said, "Your dinner's on the table whenever you're ready to eat."

"Where are you going?" came his deep voice.

"Down to the car to get your bag so I can put your things away."

"Leave it there."

She blinked. "Why?"

"Because I'm going to need it."

Hannah got this suffocating feeling in her chest. "But there are things to be washe—"

"I'll take care of them when I get to Tooele."

She followed him into the kitchen. "Surely you're not leaving for Utah so soon?"

"As a matter of fact, I'm taking off after I eat. The Jeep's loaded and ready to go. Zane's expecting me tomorrow. I've put a lot of business aside to accommodate our wedding plans, but now that we're back, I've got to get busy again."

"But you mustn't drive tonight! I know you're exhausted. You'll fall asleep at the wheel and be killed!"

His lips gave a sardonic twist. "That would solve all your problems, wouldn't it? Since the magazine was published, my net worth has increased to seventy-five billion. I think it's safe to say you and Elizabeth will be nicely taken care of."

"That's not funny!" she blurted angrily.

"Neither is marrying me under false pretenses."

While she attempted to deal with the pain from that salvo, he managed to devour his eggs and coffee in record time.

"That was delicious," he murmured as he pushed himself away from the table and rose to his considerable height. "My compliments to the chef."

This time she couldn't stop tears from forming on her lashes. "You can't go like this, Dominic."

"Can't I?" he challenged, tight-lipped.

"You *know* what I mean."

"I don't believe I've forgotten anything. Before we left for Vence, I opened up a bank account for you. It seems to me you have everything you need."

"It's our wedding night," she whispered in an aching voice.

"You want me to go to bed with you before I leave? I suppose I could do that since I paid billions for the privilege."

Each succeeding word was like a stake being pounded through her heart to her soul.

"But it wouldn't be the kind of night I

originally had in mind for us,'' he added brutally to make his point.

She clung to the counter for support. ''How long do you think you'll be gone?''

''A week at least, maybe longer. You know my cell phone number in case of an emergency. I believe that's everything.''

''No! It's not!''

She wheeled around to face him, so full of pain and hurt she didn't know where to go with it.

''Have you stopped to consider that if I were really the kind of woman who only married you to get my hands on your money, do you honestly think I wouldn't have destroyed that magazine rather than risk your finding it?

''When you came to the apartment that night, how would you have reacted if I had shown you the magazine right then? What would I have said to you?

'' 'By the way, Dominic. I just read this article and found out you're the Giraud worth seventy billion dollars. How come you didn't tell me sooner?' Of course it doesn't make any difference, because it's you I'm interested in.''

She stopped to catch her breath. ''One thing my father taught me was that it was rude to talk to anyone about how much money they made, so I refrained from discussing it with you. Any conversation of that nature should have come from you, if you had wanted to tell me.

"Since at that point in time I didn't know you wanted to marry me, I wouldn't have dared broach the subject. It wasn't any of my business."

His grim expression told her she'd gone far enough, but now that she'd got started, it was impossible to keep silent.

"Would you have believed I'd just come across that article of you that very day at Thornton's Garage? Would you have continued to go on pursuing me knowing that I knew about your background and your monetary worth?"

His cruel smile shattered her. "We'll never know the answer to that, will we."

"Oh, I think we *do* know," she countered. "I think it wouldn't have mattered when or how I told you. The result would have been the same. If anyone is hung up on money, *you* are.

"From day one I fought my attraction for you because you were so different from the other men around here. It didn't seem possible that someone like myself could interest you for more than five minutes.

"If you recall, you continued to pursue me, never once choosing to inform me who *you* really were. As soon as I accidentally found about it on my own, I tried to break things off with you."

"I noticed you didn't try very hard," he mocked. "You asked Mr. Finnegan to contact me, knowing I would come back to Laramie at the slightest provocation."

"Once you had me where you wanted me, you let it slip that you were in love with me, realizing full well that those were the words I'd been longing to hear. Your tactics were so effective, I couldn't get my ring on your finger fast enough."

"You're turning everything around." She was sounding emotional again. "I—I couldn't help telling you I loved you. It just came out."

"You're a superb actress, Hannah."

"I wasn't acting!" Her eyes blazed green fire. "I was about to make love with you, something I'd never done with another man.

"Even though I knew I wouldn't be a permanent fixture in your life, I still wanted you to realize that for me it would be the most important night of my life.

"I was madly in love with you, Dominic. I always will be. To me it was vital that I be honest about my feelings that night because I wanted you to know I didn't make such a decision lightly.''

"You mean about being a virgin. I only have your word for that, don't I?''

The pain went on and on. "That's right. It's a little matter called trust. I've had to take you on trust, too.''

"What is that supposed to mean?''

She stood her ground. "There's a lot you chose not to tell me about your past, aside from the obvious.''

Lines darkened his face. "I've shared everything of importance,'' he snapped.

"You've never told me anything about the other women in your life, and I've never pried. But it makes me think someone must have hurt you very badly.''

"On the contrary.'' His eyes became dark slits. "I've had various relationships since my twenties. Some lasted longer than others. But I never allowed any woman to become the focal point of my existence.''

"Because of the women who threw themselves at your father? Women you knew didn't love him, but were only using him for his money and the advantages he could give them?'' Her questions rang out, one after another.

"Or is it possible that somewhere in your heart of hearts, you're afraid your own mother never truly loved your father, and only married him for the money and position he could give her? Thus the reason she stayed with him all these years?

"Maybe you're afraid she's not so blameless for the breakdown of their marriage, after all, and you don't want to face it. Perhaps that's why you left France. Because you couldn't bear to be around either of them, and now you've chosen to think the worst about me!"

At this point the blood had drained out of his face.

"I'm right, aren't I!" she cried out.

"Enough!"

"I'm not through talking. You assumed that as soon as I found out who you were, I hatched some diabolical plot to ensnare the world's most eligible bachelor. Bleed him for everything I could get out of him.

"Well let me tell you something." Her voice shook. "When I read that article about you, I was frightened. Horrified even."

His expression was incredulous.

"Of course there will always be wretched women who are out for all they can get from a man, and vice versa. But I'm not one of them! You think I wanted to live in New York? You're dead wrong about that.

"I only said it because I was so afraid you would hate life here in Laramie after a while. You and I come from different worlds. You've been exposed to a great deal more of the world than most people.

"It's only natural that after a time you would feel the isolation more strongly. I didn't want to be the reason why you felt tied down to one spot. Then you would grow to hate me, and I couldn't bear that."

There was a sharp intake of breath. "If you're through, I need to get going."

Dear God. He really did know how to inflict pain.

"I'm through," came her agonized whisper. "Forgive me for saying all those awful things. Please don't leave until morning... Get a good sleep first. You can have the bed. I'll stay on the couch."

"There's no need for you to sacrifice your beauty sleep," he said in deceptively silken voice. "As a matter of fact I'm going to drive out to the property before I take off for Utah."

What? "Tonight?"

"That's right. The architect who's going to design our house needs some input. The sooner I get out there to answer a few of his questions, the sooner he can get busy drafting ideas. If I'm too tired, I'll sleep on the bunk in the museum and take off at first light.''

''But that bunk feels like a slab of rock!''

''I know exactly how it feels.''

Before she could think of another way to stop him, he'd left the apartment.

She turned toward the window. Within a minute she could see the lights from his Jeep as he backed down the private drive. The sound of the motor didn't fade until he'd moved out to the main street, distancing himself from her as fast as he could.

Tonight she understood how a person could die of heartbreak.

CHAPTER NINE

THUNDER cannonaded across the prairie. It brought wind and the smell of rain with it. Hannah had left the museum door open to breathe in the scent of sage, a reminder of Dominic and their conversation at his parents' dinner table. That event seemed like another lifetime ago.

As lightning flashed, she saw a silhouette in the entry. At first she thought—

"Hello, Hannah. Or should I say, Mrs. Giraud."

"Mr. Moench!" While she tried to recover from her disappointment that it wasn't Dominic, she moved the pile of fliers aside. "What are you doing out here on a day like this?"

"I took a lunch break to visit you. The point is, how come you're still running the museum? Now that you're married, I thought you would have hired someone else to keep it open."

Hannah avoided his inquiring look. "Dominic has had to be on the road a great deal for the last couple of weeks. The museum keeps me occupied while he's gone."

He'd told her he'd be away a week, but it had turned into fourteen long, desperately lonely days, and still there was no sign of him. Aside from the baby, work had been her salvation.

Business had brought in enough revenue that she didn't have to touch the money he'd put in the bank for her. After the things he'd said to her during their flight home from Europe, she would never access that account if she could possibly help it.

"Where's Elizabeth?"

"My friend Elaine offered to tend her today. It's her wedding present to me since she knew I needed a day to stock the museum and get Cinnamon shod."

He nodded. "How's Lisa?"

"Very happily married, thank heaven."

"I'm glad that whole situation has worked out so well."

"So am I. We've never been closer, and it's all due to you, Mr. Moench."

And Dominic.

His generosity had enabled Steve to quit one of his jobs. It also meant Lisa could start Colorado State at the end of August.

"What do you mean, me?"

"If you hadn't urged me to talk to her about adopting Elizabeth, things would have worked out very differently. You're not only an excellent attorney, but you have an amazing understanding of people, my psyche in particular."

"Thank you for those kind words, but I can't take credit for someone else's idea. It was your husband who phoned me in private and told me your life wouldn't be worth living if you couldn't adopt the baby yourself. He extracted my promise that I would talk to you about it before I did anything else."

Her hands stilled. *Dominic.* There wasn't another man to equal him. "When did he do that?" she murmured.

"On his way out of town the day you two supposedly said goodbye to each other. After he called to ask me that favor, I realized how deeply in love he was with you. He's the one with the brilliant psyche, not me."

She shook her head. "I had no idea."

"I realize that. He swore me to secrecy, but he doesn't know I'm an old family friend." He winked, then saw the moisture dusting her lashes and sobered.

"When I walked in here, I noticed you

looking mysteriously pale and far too serious for a besotted bride. Want to talk about it?''

''No, but thank you, anyway,'' she whispered.

He saw too much. Thank heaven he didn't know she hadn't seen Dominic since he'd walked out of the apartment on their wedding night. She'd been in agony ever since.

He'd called three times. The conversation centered on the baby. Hannah hadn't been able to pry any information out of him about the progress he was making on his bullet train project.

Before he hung up, he always asked her to put the receiver to Elizabeth's ear so he could tell the baby he loved her. So far he had no idea the two of them had been spending their days at the museum. For that matter he'd given no indication when he was coming home.

''I brought this.'' Mr. Moench handed her a manila envelope. ''Maybe it will help cheer you up.''

''The adoption's final?''

He smiled. ''That's right. The judge signed the papers. Everything's legal now. Elizabeth belongs to you and your husband.''

Her eyes brimmed with more tears. ''How can I ever thank you for all you've done?''

"Just be happy,"

"I am."

To know she and Dominic were the baby's parents under the law was a miracle that brought her tremendous joy.

It was the tremendous pain Dominic had inflicted she couldn't talk about, not to anyone.

His mother had phoned several times. She wanted to reminisce about the beautiful wedding, and she kept trying to get a commitment from Hannah about another visit to Vence in the near future.

Dominic's sister had made frequent phone calls, as well. Their conversation centered around the children and future family vacations together. Even Jean-Jacques had gotten in on one of the calls. His gentle teasing warmed her heart.

Everyone had been so wonderful, Hannah was compelled to keep up a happy facade for all their sakes. But she couldn't fool the old man whose compassionate glance she was still trying to avoid.

Pulling out her purse she said, "Tell me how much I owe you and I'll write you a check while you're here." She hadn't closed her account before they'd left Laramie. Now she was thankful.

He shook his head. "Your husband already paid me."

Of course.

Dominic always took care of everything.

"Hannah? If you ever need to talk, call me."

"I'll remember. Thank you."

After he dashed out to his car, which was getting a free wash, she let go with a good cry, then resumed her task of stacking fliers and refreshing her inventory. At three the rain turned to drizzle. She took advantage of the letup in the weather to get Cinnamon and bring her back to the barn.

Once that was accomplished, Hannah picked up the baby and headed home, wondering how she was going to make it through another endless evening alone. That's when she saw Dominic's Jeep in the guest parking stall. Her heart knocked against her ribs.

He must have heard her car because he opened the door of the apartment. While he moved down the steps with amazing speed, she feasted her eyes on his attractive male physique dressed in khaki pants and shirt. He would always take her breath.

Being the gentleman that he was, he opened Hannah's door first. But acute pain almost debiliatated her when he reached in the back seat for Elizabeth.

He kissed the baby's cheeks and neck until she was making those happy sounds only he could elicit. After reaching for the diaper bag, he proceeded to carry her up to the apartment. Hannah followed at a discreet distance.

"It's about time *ma fille* came home to her *papa*. I have plans for us this evening, *mignonne*."

As Hannah shut the door, he eyed her dispassionately. "Where have you been?"

With that question, any hope that their two week separation might have softened him a little bit was dashed. She bit her lip so she wouldn't cry out in a blind rage.

"At work, like you." Miraculously her voice remained steady.

His jaw hardened. "I bought the property so you could stay at home and be a full-time mother to Elizabeth. I don't want you or the baby out at the museum anymore.

"Tomorrow we'll put an ad in the newspaper for someone to run it. Preferably a retired person who likes people and wants something interesting to do with his time until it gets too cold out there."

That was exactly the kind of person Hannah had pictured running the museum.

"Once he's hired, I'll have to spend a few days out there training him."

"Of course. As soon as that day arrives, I'll make arrangements to stay home and take care of Elizabeth." He blew on her tummy until the laughter rolled out of her. When Hannah saw him smile at the baby in response, her insides melted.

"Does she need a bottle right now?"

"No, not until bed."

"Good. I thought we'd go swimming."

"*Swimming*— Now?"

"That's right. The Executive Inn has an indoor pool and a small, heated wading pool for children."

There was this suffocating feeling in her chest. "I don't t-think—that is, neither the baby or I even own a—"

"If you're worried about suits," he broke in smoothly, "you don't need to be. In anticipation of our spending time together, I bought one for you and the baby in the hotel gift shop. Swimming with Elizabeth is one activity I've been eager to do with her."

Hannah clung to the nearest chair back for support. "I'm sure she'll love it."

"You sound as if you're not coming with us." When next she looked at him, she couldn't understand the strange bleakness mixed with some other unnamed emotion coming from his eyes. "I've been away for a while and would prefer you to be there in case the baby suddenly gets frightened."

Naturally that was the only reason he wanted her at the pool with them. There were times like now when she wished she'd called the police that night to report a horn honking out on her property. Then she would never have laid eyes on him, never would have known this excruciating kind of one-sided heartache.

"Of course I'll come and watch."

"But you won't swim."

"Not tonight."

As long as you continue to believe I betrayed you, there can be no joy in anything.

His gaze made an impersonal perusal of her face and figure before it landed on the envelope she was holding.

"What's that?"

Hannah averted her eyes before handing it to him. She wouldn't be able to handle their travesty of marriage much longer if she was always going to be suspect in his eyes.

"While you open it, I'll freshen up and meet you at the car."

A few minutes later, dressed in clean jeans and a pullover, she hurried out of the apartment and down the stairs. He reached across her to shut her car door. The slight contact of his hair-roughened arm against her chest set her body on fire.

Perhaps he was gripped by the same raw tension because they drove to the hotel in relative silence. As soon as they reached the pool area beyond some double doors, he handed her the baby and a sack.

"The suits are inside. Why don't you get hers on while I change. I'll meet you out here in a few minutes."

Without waiting for a response, he left her to deal with Elizabeth.

"Come on. Let's find a place to get you undressed. In a few minutes you're going to have your first swimming lesson," she murmured to the baby.

Hannah readjusted the diaper bag on her shoulder, then headed for the far end of the room while Elizabeth's golden head kept swinging around in an attempt to find Dominic.

The kiddie pool lay beyond the shallow end of the large pool. She noticed several sets of families, mothers and fathers playing in the water with their children. Her eyes misted over.

Did they have any idea how lucky they

were to all belong to each other, let alone enjoy each other's company?

She tore her eyes from the scene and lay Elizabeth on one of the lounging chairs where she could change her into the dainty one-piece outfit he'd purchased. The suit had a blue baby whale motif and tied at the shoulders with shoestring straps.

Dominic, who had impeccable taste and made anything he wore look fantastic, had an eye for what looked good, even for a baby. Out of curiosity she peeked at the other suit. It was a black bikini. This was the type of suit her father would never have allowed, but it was exactly the kind of thing Lisa would have picked to thwart him.

Hannah, on the other hand, would wear it if she were swimming privately with her husband, but she would never expose her body like that in public. In the past she'd confined herself to a modest one-piece suit. Well-endowed like her mother, she felt far too self-conscious to swim in anything more revealing.

Thank goodness she'd already told Dominic she wouldn't be swimming tonight. Heat swept up her body to scorch her face when she thought of having to wear two skimpy pieces of material in front of him. It would be different if he still looked at her with love.

Putting the sack and its contents aside, she concentrated on getting Elizabeth's diaper changed before she put her in the new suit.

"It's a perfect fit and you look adorable!" She kissed the baby's nose and carried her over to the edge of the wading pool. The water felt warm to her fingers. "You're going to love this, Elizabeth."

"So am I," a deep, familiar male voice spoke directly behind her. Hannah turned her head in time to see Dominic step in the water and walk over to them.

He must have taken a swim in the big pool first. Like some Greek god rising out of the sea, water had sleeked back his dark brown hair, defining a faint widow's peak. Droplets of moisture clung to the bronzed skin of his hard-muscled frame. Dark hair dusted his chest and arrowed beneath the waistband of his trunks.

Once again his male beauty hit Hannah like a physical force. She could hardly breathe. Until he spoke to the baby in French, not even Elizabeth was sure what to do in front of this magnificent male specimen who got down on his knees to put her in the water with him.

She didn't cry. She simply stared at him in awe, exactly the way Hannah was doing until she caught herself. Quickly she moved to bring a chair closer to the edge of the pool where she could watch.

Slowly he swirled the baby around on her back. Every time he let a few drops of water tickle her face, she laughed out loud. "You like that, don't you, *Petite*."

The absolute trust in those baby eyes focused entirely on him brought a devastating smile to his lips, and a lump to Hannah's throat.

He used to smile at me like that… The ache in her heart deepened until she moaned from the pain of it. She had no idea how she was going to get through tonight when separate sleeping arrangements would have to be made.

Unlike his mother, Hannah knew she couldn't live in a marriage where she was estranged from her husband. If Dominic didn't come around soon, then it was only a matter of time before she went to Mr. Moench to start divorce proceedings. The whole ugly issue over visitation would have to be sorted out.

How tragic to be thinking this way when

only today the attorney had handed her Elizabeth's adoption papers.

The baby adored her new daddy, and he loved her. The bond between them was a beautiful thing to witness. Right now they were both having a wonderful time. He'd been teaching Elizabeth to kick her legs. In fact he'd done such a good job of urging her on, she repeatedly splashed water in his face. His full-bodied laughter revealed the measure of his enjoyment.

Finally Hannah pulled a receiving blanket out of the diaper bag and walked over to the edge. "I hate to break this up, but it's long past Elizabeth's bedtime."

Dominic's head reared back. Their eyes made contact. "Is it that late already?"

"You two have been having so much fun, you must have lost track of the time. While I get her dressed, why don't you do a few laps in the big pool?"

Through shuttered eyes he said, "That might be a good idea. Here you go, *mignonne*. Back to your mommy."

He lifted a slippery wet Elizabeth so Hannah could wrap her in the blanket. In a couple of swift strides he dove into the other pool with the speed of a torpedo.

By the time Dominic met them ten minutes

later, Elizabeth had finally settled down in her car seat with a bottle. Out of the corner of her eye Hannah noticed he'd put on a T-shirt in a slate-blue color. He'd come straight from the shower. She could detect the faint scent of lime.

Good heavens. He looked and smelled too wonderful! Unconsciously she gripped the sides of her seat with both hands. This outing had been a mistake.

Dominic levered himself into the driver's seat. ''I brought some preliminary renderings from the architect with me. Before you fall asleep tonight, I'd like you to look them over and see if there's anything that pleases you. He expects us to make corrections and additions, so feel free to write on the drawings.''

Hannah had been listening to him, but all she heard was, *Before you fall asleep.*

He couldn't have made it any plainer that he was staying in this marriage for Elizabeth's sake only. Obviously two weeks of being apart from Hannah had solidified his intention to imitate his parents' lifestyle, one she abhorred and wanted no part of.

But she held back from saying anything until after they'd reached the apartment and Dominic had put the baby down for the night with her bottle. When he came into the living room a little while later, Hannah was waiting for him on the couch.

He stood at his full height with his hands on his hips, his gaze flicking to the large tube on the coffee table. "You haven't unrolled the drawings yet. No other woman of my acquaintance would have been able to contain her curiosity by now."

Another dagger pierced her heart.

"But I'm not like any of the women you've known," she answered quietly. "As for looking at those blueprints, there's no point."

His eyebrows became a dark slash of mockery. "At last you admit you had a different dream."

She nodded. "I admit it. But as you say, it was only a dream. There was no substance, after all, so it shouldn't come as any surprise that I'm divorcing you, Dominic."

His body stilled in place.

"I've had two weeks to think, and I take full blame for the failure of our marriage. I should have talked to you about that magazine article as soon as I saw it.

"Naturally any man or woman who has come from a background like yours has to be constantly on the alert for fortune hunters. Jean-Jacques told me Nicole proposed to him because he was afraid she would think he wanted her money if he asked her to marry him.

"With hindsight I can see it makes perfect sense. When you learned I'd commited the sin of omission, you had every right to think the worst about me, especially considering my meager circumstances.

"I understand why you've lost trust in me, so I'm going to give you back your freedom. The property has already been sold to you. It's yours to do with as you please. Elizabeth and I will continue to live in this apartment. You'll always be her daddy and you can see her whenever you like.

"There's an ad in the paper placed by a couple that needs a nanny during the work week for their one-year-old boy. If they brought him here, I could tend him while I raise Elizabeth. Not only will she have a friend, I'll be able to stay home with my daughter and earn my keep.

"Knowing you, I realize you'll want to pay for all the baby's expenses. That's fine. When I see Mr. Moench in the morning, I'll tell him not to make any proviso for alimony. It goes without saying you'll have unlimited visitation rights."

She pulled the rings off her finger and

placed them next to the tube. "There. In some communities of the world, all we would have to say is, 'We are no longer married,' and it would be done."

Reaching for her purse, she got to her feet. "Unfortunately in this country we live under laws that make divorce so much more complicated. However in *our* case we shouldn't have any problem because we haven't consummated our marriage. Therefore a simple annulment ought to hurry up the process."

Before he could guess her intentions she moved to the door and opened it. "Tonight I'm going to stay at Elaine's house. If there's an emergency, her number is on the paper next to the phone in the kitchen. I'll be back in the morning before you take off again for parts unknown. Goodnight."

Maybe she heard him call out her name, but she'd already flown down the stairs and had started her car. If Elizabeth hadn't been inside the apartment, Hannah had no doubts he would have come after her and prevented her from walking out on him.

As it was, he'd been trapped by circumstances beyond on his control and forced to spend the night pondering the fact that not all women were like his mother. This woman wasn't willing to stay in a bad marriage.

Bad marriage?

Hannah let out an angry laugh. She and Dominic didn't have a marriage. Period!

"Hannah?"

Someone was calling to her from the museum doorway. She turned her head.

"Alik?"

If he was here, that meant Dominic was probably outside. Hannah was so shocked to see him, she almost fell off the chair. Thanks to his swift reflexes, she reached the floor without breaking a leg.

"Thank you," she whispered shakily.

"Are you all right?"

"Yes." *But she wasn't.* "I-is Dominic with you?"

"No. I was hoping to find him here."

Part of her felt relief because she couldn't bear another tension-filled confrontation with him. But another part was shattered.

She hadn't seen her husband since that ghastly dawn when she'd come home from Elaine's over a week ago. Without saying a word, he'd stormed out of her living room and had taken off in the Jeep. He'd left her rings and the tube of drawings untouched on the coffee table.

While she'd hurried to check on the baby

who was still asleep in the crib, she'd heard the squeal of his tires even though he was several blocks away.

"I had no idea you'd driven up in front."

"I called to you several times, but you were miles away." Heat crept up her neck and cheeks. "Where's the little angel? I've been looking forward to playing with her."

"She's home with my sister." Her voice trembled.

His glance darted to the saddle blanket dangling over her arm. "Do you want some help with that?"

"Oh, no, but thank you anyway. I'm through dismantling the walls now."

He looked perplexed. "Why are you doing that?"

"I'm starting a new job soon, so I came out here to close down the museum for the winter. Since that would have been impossible with the baby around, I asked Lisa to tend her."

"What new job?" he demanded, sounding very much like Dominic just then.

She averted her eyes. "I thought Dominic would have told you."

He rubbed his chest absently. "Neither Zane nor I have had contact with him in a while. He told us he had to fly to Europe on private family business. I thought he'd be back home by now.''

Dominic was in France?

The hollow in her heart deepened. That could only mean one thing. He'd wanted to tell his mother about their divorce in person.

''Dominic was here a little over a week ago. He stayed one night, then left the next morning. I guess he drove straight to the Denver airport.''

Alik's eyes surveyed her with grave concern. ''Please don't take this the wrong way, but you look like you've really been through it. What's wrong, Hannah? You can talk to me. I assure you it won't go any further.''

She did know that.

There was no use trying to hide the truth from him. He was one of Dominic's best friends and would learn about it soon enough.

''We're getting a divorce. I went to see my attorney a few days ago.''

''Oh, no.''

The next thing she knew Alik had put his arms around her. His compassion opened the floodgates. As he rocked her back and forth, she found herself telling him everything.

When she finally realized what a scene she was making, she backed away from him and wiped her eyes with the backs of her hands.

"I'm sorry I broke down like that." To cover her embarrassment, she started stacking the rest of the wall plaques into cartons she'd brought from the grocery store.

Grim-faced, he began helping her. "Dominic's a damn fool. But that's because he's so deeply in love with you. One day soon he'll wake up, Hannah."

"You don't know that."

He put his hands on her upper arms to still them. "Yes, I do. Because I know his heart, and now I know yours. Come on. Let's finish up here, then I'm taking you to dinner."

She let out a weary sigh. "I won't say no to that."

"Good." He flashed her an encouraging smile before they filled one box and began on another. As he reached for a fresh stack of plaques, he suddenly broke into laughter.

It made her smile in spite of her pain. "What?"

"I've got to have this one for my trailer. I think I'll nail it to the door."

Hannah glanced at it.

"'My good man, could you tell me where your boss is?'" The Wyoming cowboy glared back at the Easterner, spit out his tobacco and said, "'The son of a bitch ain't been born yet!'"

"This is one of my favorites, too. It sells out constantly."

"How much do I owe you for it?"

"For you, it's free. While we're at it, why don't you give Zane this old map of the Pony Express. It might have sentimental value for him since he's from San Francisco."

"Can I have one like it, too?"

"You can have anything you want, with my blessing."

She'd been prepared to like Alik and Zane because they were Dominic's friends. But not until today did she realize how really special they were.

Alik had shown up at the museum during one of her darkest hours. Though she believed her marriage to Dominic was over, she loved Alik for asking her not to give up on it.

With another pair of hands to help, her work was done in short order. She eventually stood up and turned around. "I think that's it, thanks to you."

"Happy to oblige. Shall I take these boxes out to your car?"

"If you don't mind, I'd be very grateful. Here are the keys."

While he was outside, her cell phone rang.

On cue her heart began to thud sickeningly. *Dominic?*

She raised the phone to her ear and said hello, praying to hear the sound of his voice. It had been so long...

CHAPTER TEN

"HI, HONEY. It's Colleen!"

Hannah's eyes widened in surprise. "Colleen! How are you?"

"I'm fine, but there's trouble and I'm calling out the Brigade."

"What's wrong?"

"A lost child up in the Snowy Range area near the Libby Flats Wildflower Trail. I'll tell everyone the particulars when we meet. How soon can you get to my ranch?"

"I'll be over as soon as I find a sitter for Elizabeth."

"Knew I could count on you, honey."

The second Hannah got off the phone, she told Alik she would have to take a rain check on their dinner. After she explained about the emergency, he told her he would finish up and lock the museum. They could meet at the Executive Inn later that night, or talk in the morning.

Giving him a kiss and hug, she saddled

Cinnamon, then hitched the trailer to her car and loaded her horse.

On the way back to Laramie, she phoned Lisa to tell her what had happened. Hannah was about to say that she would call Elaine to see if she would tend the baby, but Lisa interrupted her and volunteered to stay with Elizabeth for as long as necessary.

Relieved on several counts, Hannah drove straight to Colleen's ranch where at least thirty of the women had already assembled.

"There's no time to lose," she heard their captain say. "As soon as we get to our destination, grab a walkie-talkie from the back of my truck so we can stay in touch. I'll relay any news to the person in charge of the search and rescue, as well as the rangers.

"Remember—there's a forest fire blazing in the next range over, so there's going to be a lot of smoke. Don't do anything foolish. We're looking for a five-year-old boy named Tommy Boyle from Florida who's never been in the mountains before and has wandered away from a family reunion picnic this morning. His parents are frantic.

"He's of average height and build, and has brown hair and eyes. He's wearing denims and a light blue T-shirt that has a Star Wars logo. All right. That's it. Let's pull out!"

The thought of Elizabeth ever being lost in the wilderness was too awful to contemplate. She knew every woman there who had children of her own was thinking the same thing. Surely with all this help they could find the boy.

But half an hour into the mountain camping area, Hannah wasn't as certain. The low cloud ceiling and smoke from the fire made for poor visibility.

"We'll make a sweep, proceeding away from the campground at twenty yards apart. Let's go!" Colleen blew her whistle and everyone began walking their horses.

Hannah glanced at her watch. It was nearing three o'clock. They had five hours of daylight left. "Come on, Cinnamon. Let's see what we can find."

They swept one area for an hour, then another, passing through spruce and fir trees. Two more hours passed. Nothing. At one point Cinnamon lowered her head to drink from a small mountain stream. It gave Hannah an idea.

She rode over to Wilma. "I'm going to follow the stream down the mountain. Little kids love to float things. Maybe that's what Tommy did."

"You'd better not, Hannah. The smoke's getting worse. Colleen wouldn't approve."

"She'll never know if you don't tell her."

They two women stared hard at each other. "I'll come with you."

"No. Someone has to cover your area and mine now."

"You're right. I'll do it. But don't go for more than a half hour before you head back to the campground."

"I won't."

"Good luck."

When a physically and emotionally exhausted Dominic pulled into the drive leading to the apartment, he was surprised to see an old pickup truck parked in Hannah's usual spot. Her compact car was nowhere in sight.

Frowning, he levered himself from the Jeep and took the stairs three at a time. He didn't know who was more surprised when he unlocked the door and pushed it open to discover a contented Elizabeth on the floor with a younger version of Hannah who hurriedly got to her bare feet.

He'd seen pictures of her, but looking at her in person made him realize how closely she and his wife resembled each other. Both were raving beauties. No wonder he'd thought the baby was Hannah's when he'd first met her.

"Forgive me for startling you, Lisa. I'm Dominic Giraud, Hannah's husband."

"I know who you are." The baby had inherited her sunny smile. "It looks like Elizabeth does, too." His heart melted when he saw how eagerly his adorable daughter reached for him.

"*Petite,*" he whispered into the baby's sweet-smelling neck. "You've grown while I've been gone! Do you know how much I've missed you?" He kissed her cheeks and tummy until she laughed out loud. "I swear I'm never staying away from you this long again."

He'd known before he left Wyoming that the only thing in the world that mattered to him was right here in Laramie. But Hannah's determination to divorce him had been so swift and devastating, he'd reeled from the possibility that she might really have meant it.

In his grief, he'd flown to Antibes to be with his sister. She was the one person who understood his demons because she'd battled them herself over the years. Through their long talks she helped him throw off the dreaded blackness of their family's pain, something that had been eating him alive since his teens.

Jean-Jacques told him he'd better fly home as fast as he could and get down on his knees to Hannah. Forget his Gallic pride.

Dominic was more than prepared to do that. As he'd found out in recent months, life had no meaning without her.

He turned his head in Lisa's direction. "Where's your sister?"

"I tended the baby while Hannah closed up the museum today."

Thank God she'd followed through on that plan at least.

"While she was out there, she got a call from the brigade. Someone's child is missing and there's a forest fire raging. Hannah hasn't come home yet. I told her I'd stay with Elizabeth for as long as it took."

He felt sickness in his gut. "Is there a number to reach her?"

"You might do better to call the police or fire department for details. Hannah said every available person was out helping with the search."

His adrenaline started to kick in. "Is this a normal activity for the brigade?"

She nodded. "They always assist in emergencies. Some, like Hannah, have been trained to serve as volunteer firefighters.''

"Hannah does that?" he exploded as horrifying pictures filled his mind.

"Until she got saddled with my problems, she led an amazing life. If you ever saw her ride broncos, or slalom ski or paddle a kayak in white water, you'd realize she does a lot of scary things. But she probably hasn't told you the half because she's so modest. Hannah's nothing like me.''

His alarm had reached its zenith. "Lisa— would you mind looking after Elizabeth a little longer? I've got to go find my wife!"

"Steve's visiting his folks in Grand Junction, so I'm prepared to stay all night if necessary. I know you're in a hurry, but I want to thank you for the money you sent us. It was very generous and made all the difference.''

"It was my pleasure." He gave the baby another kiss and lay her on the quilt. "I'll be back, *mignonne*.''

"Tommy? Tommy Boyle? If you can hear me, shout as loud as you can!"

Hannah's surefooted mare continued down the side of the stream, sometimes walking in the water, sometimes in the wild grass. The smell of smoke in her nostrils was growing stronger. Another five minutes and it would be too dark to continue the search.

Every few seconds she stopped to listen. The forest was alive with sounds, but nothing human. Expelling a frustrated sigh, she had no choice but to head back to the campground. Maybe he'd already been found.

But in case he was out here somewhere, she called his name at regular intervals, then waited for an answer. Halfway to her destination Cinnamon stopped for another drink. That's when she heard a different sound.

"Tommy? Is that you?"

"Mom?" came a frightened little voice a few yards to her right.

Thank God. "My name's Hannah! I've come to take you to your parents."

"M-my leg's b-bleeding."

"Don't worry. I'll take care of you. Just keep talking until I find you."

"Is the f-fire going to g-get us?"

"That's just smoke. The fire's far away," she lied. "I've got a horse and we'll be out of here in just a minute. Now I can see you." The boy had crouched under a huge pine tree.

She jumped off Cinnamon and ran over to him. Blood was oozing out of a gash on his lower leg where his pants were torn. There was nothing for it but to take off her blouse to prevent any more seepage. Then she picked him up and sat him on her horse before climbing behind him.

"Here we go, Tommy."

The fire was definitely closer. While she urged Cinnamon to walk as fast as she could through the dense forest, Hannah got on her walkie-talkie.

"Colleen? This is Hannah. I've found the boy. He's got a gash on his leg and has lost some blood, but he's all right. We're moving upstream, about ten minutes from the campground."

"Good for you, honey, but you can't come that way. The wind changed and the fire's too close. Can you make it from where are you to old fire road due north?"

"Yes." At least I'm saying that now.

"We'll see you there in a few minutes."

"Did you hear that, Tommy?" Hannah said as they headed north. He didn't answer. No doubt he was in shock.

"Okay, Cinnamon. I'm depending on you to get us out of here." With a pat to her flank, the horse took off. It was getting difficult to breathe.

Hannah tried to remember the rules she'd learned in fire training about avoiding panic.

She couldn't think of one. She wanted Dominic. She would dream about him. He'd make everything all right. He always made everything all right.

Dominic honked at a couple of rangers blocking the mountain road. Instead of getting out of the way, they walked up to his Jeep.

"Sorry, sir, but no more vehicles are allowed past this point because of the fire."

"Please—the people at the campground said my *wife's* on that mountain!" Dominic cried out. He could see licks of flame destroying larger swatches of forest below the ridge. *Mon Dieu.* If anything happened to her...

"We understand how you feel, but this is for your protection. Stay back and let the firefighters do their job."

Muttering a string of profanity in his native tongue, he leaped from the seat and started running.

"Hey—you're not permitted in there!"

But Dominic wasn't listening as he made his way through the long line of emergency vehicles on both sides of the narrow dirt road. Smoke filled his nostrils as he raced to the front of the line.

A group of emergency crews from the

paramedic's truck were huddled a few yards away.

He grabbed one of them by the shoulder. "Has there been any sign of my wife yet? She's got the lost boy with her."

The other man shook his head. "Not yet."

Terrified by that news, Dominic let go of him and started down the slope. "Hannah!" he cried at the top of his lungs. But before he could shout her name again, he was dragged back by two of the men.

"You can't go down there. It's too dangerous. She should be showing up any minute now."

He strained against them, but they restrained him. Tears welled in his eyes. *"Dear God,"* Dominic prayed. "You can't take her from me now. *Hannah! Hannah!"*

She had to be hallucinating.

Dominic wasn't in Laramie, but it sounded like his voice calling to her in the near darkness.

"I can see you, *mon amour*. Just a few more feet up the slope."

Nothing seemed real until the horse made a mighty leap onto the road. The boy seemed to slide right away from her, and then she felt her body being pulled from the saddle into a familiar pair of arms.

It *was* Dominic.

She would know his body anywhere, the scent of his skin, the heavy tattoo of his heart.

He carried her like a baby and kept whispering her name.

When she heard the word "ambulance," she clung fiercely to his neck. "I don't need one," she cried between coughs. "It's the boy who's hurt, and Cinnamon needs looking after."

"Dieu merci," She heard his voice repeat the words feverishly. "They're both being taken care of, my love."

Choking made it difficult to talk, but she managed to beg, "Please don't make me go to the hospital. Just take me home."

As if by magic she felt herself being carried a long distance, then deposited in a car which turned out to be Dominic's Jeep.

She watched in a daze as he tore off his T-shirt and helped her into it. Not until then did she remember removing her blouse to stem the boy's bleeding.

"Domin—"

"Don't talk now, Hannah," he ordered in a fierce tone. "Not until I get you out of this smoke."

The rangers waved him on as he backed around and started down the mountain road. When they came to the campground, he pulled to the side of the road for a moment.

"Here, darling. Drink this." He cradled the back of her head to help her swallow.

"Oh...that water tastes divine." She found herself gulping down every drop. Through shuttered eyelids she could see the tension in his tanned face, the strained cords in his neck.

"After the harrowing ordeal you've just lived through, you need rest and care."

This was the old Dominic, the man she'd fallen in love with. Without his shirt he looked like he had that evening in the hotel pool when he'd emerged from the water like some magnificent god of the sea. She moaned in reaction.

"Hannah?" he cried, sounding unbelievably alarmed as he smoothed the curls from her forehead. She'd never known him to display this kind of vulnerability before. It was a revelation to her.

"I'm all right, Dominic," she said between coughs. "It's just that the water tasted so good. Please—let's get out of here." Tears beaded her lashes. "I just want to be alone with you."

"It's all I've ever wanted," he muttered beneath his breath, and turned on the motor.

The Jeep seemed to have wings. Before long she could tell they'd left the mountains because the air no longer smelled of acrid smoke. Her lungs couldn't seem to get enough oxygen.

But with every breath of fresh air reviving her a little more, it also made her more cognizant of the fact that Dominic had actually returned to Laramie.

"I don't want to hear how long you're staying this time. Just promise you won't leave me tonight."

A stream of something unintelligible poured from his lips. "I'm home for as long as you need me, Hannah."

Her eyes closed tightly. She had difficulty swallowing. "That's a long time. But I don't have the right to ask it of you."

He made a sound as if he'd had all he could take. "You have every right," he ground out. "You're my wife! I want no other."

"But will you ever be able to trust me again?" She was struggling for breath now, and it wasn't all due to the smoke. "After what you told me about your father hoping I was a mercenary woman only out for what I could get from you so he could gloat, I realized you've had to live your whole life with the fear of not being loved for yourself. It's no wonder you felt betrayed when you found that magazine.''

She buried her face in her hands. "I've gone over it and over it, but every time I find myself wishing you didn't have that kind of money, I have to remember that we would never have met otherwise.

"Then I love your money, and I'm so thankful that you are who you are, I wouldn't want one single thing changed about you.'' After wiping her eyes, she lifted her head. "Forgive me for hurting you, Dominic.''

The Jeep came to a sudden stop. Before she could countenance it, he'd put one arm around the back of her seat, and cupped her face with the other.

Forcing her to look at him, he said, "I'm the one who needs to ask your forgiveness.'' Incredibly she saw tears in those dark brown depths, a sight she never expected to see. "I came back to Laramie to beg you to hear me out and give me a second chance to be the husband I always wanted to be to you.

"If anyone is guilty of making mistakes, blame me for not telling you the truth about myself the first time you asked me what I did for a living. But the amazing way you and I met, the instant bond that sprang up between the baby and me, all seemed part of the enchantment.

"After the women I've known—to meet anyone as adorable and wonderful and refreshing as you, I didn't want to ruin it by talking about myself. But not even I knew the measure of my entrancement until I thought your love might not be real.

"Hannah—I've suffered pain and disappointment in my life, but I've never experienced the firsthand sensation of going into shock.

"When I thought you didn't love me, someone might just as well have stabbed me repeatedly in the gut and left me to die."

"Oh, darling—" She hid her face in his neck.

"That night before our wedding, I sat there for hours next to Elizabeth without moving. Like shards of shattered crystal exploding in every direction, bits and pieces of our miraculous courtship seemed to lay heaped around me. Broken splinters that could never be mended to resemble the glory of a love I thought was our destiny."

She held him tighter to stop his trembling. "Can you ever forgive my cruelty to you?

Mon Dieu!, Hannah—have I killed that precious thing between us. I love you, darling."

Dominic needed more than words. Hannah lifted her mouth to his, pouring all the emotion of body and soul into that swirling vortex of unending ecstasy.

Time was no longer relevant as they shared their mutual hunger for each other. Without his shirt, she was free to explore his hair-roughened chest which was hot to the touch. Everywhere her lips caressed, she heard him groan in need. Then he was touching her, loving her, producing sensations that left her begging for more until she was a writhing supplicant.

"Hannah—" His voice sounded ragged as he eventually disengaged himself from her arms. "A man can only take so much. Stay over on your side of the car and don't come near me until we're back at the apartment. I'm going to ask for your promise on that." His magnificent chest was heaving from the force of his emotions before he started the car.

Realizing the power she had over him, she settled back with a wicked smile. In a few minutes she would be able to love him all night long and he would receive the answer he was looking for until every last demon had been conquered.

Hannah awoke to an unfamiliar weight across her legs and chest. Dominic was in a deep sleep, his right hand still tangled in her hair. In the obscure morning light she could just make out the firm line of his nose, the shape of his compelling male mouth and proud jaw.

All these weeks of imagining making love with her husband had been one thing. But to finally know his full possession transcended every other experience of her life.

There weren't words.

If it were possible, she could lie in his arms forever and never tire of the pleasure they gave each other. Heat swept over her in waves when she realized her needs had been insatiable. But then, so had his...

It came as a shock to discover she had such a passionate side to her nature. One he insisted, flashing her a devilish smile, he'd always known had existed, and had been impatiently waiting to awaken.

A thrill of desire shot through her system. He'd awakened her, all right. Now it was time to waken him, before the baby started making noises.

Last night Lisa had offered to stay and take

care of Elizabeth so Hannah and Dominic could sleep in late. But Dominic confided that he wanted his family to himself, so Lisa left promising to get together with them soon.

"Bonjour, mon amour," she whispered in his ear, anxious to speak the same kind of endearments he used with her. *"Je t'aime."*

She was looking into his eyes when they opened. The fire she'd seen in them last night burned hotter than ever. His hand reached out to pull her head toward him.

"Kiss me, so I know you're real."

She was eager to obey his command, but *he* was the one who captured her mouth and took them to the dizzying heights of rapture only two people who loved as they did could know.

Much later he moved her on top of him, but instead of the eager, tremulous face of joy, his expression had sobered. She couldn't imagine.

"Last night, when I learned you had gone in the forest to save that boy knowing both of you were in danger of being burned alive, I died a second death. Promise me you'll never do anything that heroic again, Hannah. My heart couldn't take it."

He meant what he said. She could feel it.

"I promise. You're too important to me to

do anything that could jeopardize the time we have together.''

He kissed her deeply. ''To wake up to you makes me realize I never want to wake up again without you right here like this. Do you thin—''

''Yes, my darling.'' She had anticipated the question he was asking. ''I want to love you every single morning of our lives, too. In fact I can't wait to help you with your project.

''If we bought a motor home, it could pull your Jeep, and we could travel the rest of the country together. We'd get twice the work done in half the time. Elizabeth will love it because she'll get to be with her daddy on a twenty-four hour basis. And I'll love it because I'll be able to love you and care for you all night, every night.''

Light flared in the recesses of his eyes. ''You really mean that don't you?''

''With all my heart, Dominic.''

He grasped one of her hands and kissed it. ''What about your studies?''

''As important as they are, they can wait. There's something much more vital at stake right now.''

''What's that?'' he whispered.

''Working on a little sister or brother for Elizabeth. If she remains our only child, she'll be so spoiled by your love, she'll be impossible to live with. The sooner we have another baby for you to dote on, the sooner she'll get over her jealousy.''

The smile she craved broke out on his bronzed face. ''You think she loves me that much?''

''I refuse to answer such a foolish question. If you can't remember the way she flung her little body to get into your arms, *I* can.''

Laughter burst out of him. The full-bodied kind that shook her and the bed. ''I guess those rodeo moves are an intrinsic part of the Carr genes.''

Hannah smiled mysteriously. ''I suppose we'll have to wait and find out after baby number two arrives.''

He eyed her passionately. ''I hope I've already made you pregnant.''

''You couldn't want that as much as I do.'' Her voice caught.

He kissed her neck and shoulders. ''You promised to tell me what you told Elizabeth the night I was carted away to the hospital. How long do I have to remain in suspense before I hear the details?''

''I thought I told you everything you wanted to know in the middle of the night.''

''I want to hear it again, *mon amour*.''

"Have you no shame?"

"None. Come closer. You're too far away."

"First, I have to do something."

One dark brow lifted in query. "What would that be?"

"I have to make a phone call."

"Now?" He sounded hurt.

"I'm afraid so."

With great difficulty she reached across his body for the phone and dialed information. "I need the number of the Executive Inn, please."

Dominic raised up on one elbow and looked down at her, his lambent brown eyes questioning.

She lifted a hand to trace the masculine line of his mouth with her index finger. He was such a beautiful man, she made a little sound of pleasure in her throat. "In due time all will be revealed, my love."

"Mr. Alik Jarman, please. I don't know his room number."

Dominic looked incredulous. "He's here in Laramie?"

As soon as she heard his friend's voice answer the phone she said, "Alik? It's Hannah." Suddenly tears filled her eyes and her throat closed up. "You were right about everything. Dominic came home from Vence last night. He's here next to me, and wants to talk to you.''

The next few minutes filled Hannah with quiet joy as her husband related the highlights of the rescue to his friend. He kept kissing her in between sentences.

''Hannah was the heroine, but proud as I am of her, I'm never letting her out of my sight again. In case I didn't say it before, I want to thank you and Zane for putting up with me the night before the wedding. I couldn't have made it through without my friends.''

''*What?*'' Hannah cried softly, wondering what exactly he'd done after leaving Elizabeth's room.

His eyes held a mysterious gleam. ''Hannah's part of our bullet train team now, but first we're going to take a long-overdue honeymoon. In fact it started last night so I'm going to sign off now. Tell Zane I'll be in touch later.

''*Much much later,*'' he murmured against her mouth while his hand struggled to put the receiver back on the hook.

HARLEQUIN ◆ PRESENTS®

The world's bestselling romance series...
The series that brings you your favorite authors,
month after month:

Helen Bianchin...Emma Darcy
Lynne Graham...Penny Jordan
Miranda Lee...Sandra Morton
Anne Mather...Carole Mortimer
Susan Napier...Michelle Reid

and many more uniquely talented authors!

Wealthy, powerful, gorgeous men...
Women who have feelings just like your own...
The stories you love, set in exotic, glamorous locations...

HARLEQUIN PRESENTS,
Seduction and passion guaranteed!

Visit us at www.eHarlequin.com   HPGEN00

Harlequin® Historical

From rugged lawmen and
valiant knights to defiant heiresses
and spirited frontierswomen,
Harlequin Historicals will
capture your imagination with
their dramatic scope, passion
and adventure.

Harlequin Historicals...
they're too good to miss!

HHGENR

HARLEQUIN®
Makes any time special.™

Upbeat, all-American romances about the pursuit of love, marriage and family.

Duets™
Two brand-new, full-length romantic comedy novels for one low price.

Harlequin® Historical
Rich and vivid historical romances that capture the imagination with their dramatic scope, passion and adventure.

Temptation™
Sexy, sassy and seductive— Temptation is hot sizzling romance.

SUPERROMANCE
A bigger romance read with more plot, more story-line variety, more pages and a romance that's evocatively explored.

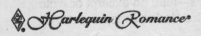
Harlequin Romance®
Love stories that capture the essence of traditional romance.

INTRIGUE®
Dynamic mysteries with a thrilling combination of breathtaking romance and heart-stopping suspense.

HARLEQUIN PRESENTS®
Meet sophisticated men of the world and captivating women in glamorous, international settings.

Visit us at www.eHarlequin.com

HGEN00

Your Romantic Books—find them at

www.eHarlequin.com

Visit the *Author's Alcove*

➤ Find the most complete information anywhere
on your favorite author.

➤ Try your hand in the Writing Round Robin—
contribute a chapter to an online book in the
making.

Enter the *Reading Room*

➤ Experience an interactive novel—help determine
the fate of a story being created now by one of
your favorite authors.

➤ Join one of our reading groups and discuss your
favorite book.

Drop into *Shop eHarlequin*

➤ Find the latest releases—read an excerpt or write
a review for this month's Harlequin top sellers.

➤ Try out our amazing search feature—tell us your
favorite theme, setting or time period and we'll find
a book that's perfect for you.

All this and more available at

www.eHarlequin.com
on Women.com Networks

HEYRB1